GOOGOLPLEX

KG JOHANSSON

I will make you to be the first of all living creatures.

Inscription at the death temple of Hatshepsut, Deir-el Bahri

1

In the beginning, there was nothing, but since nothing was, he didn't know. Not until time began, in that first moment where a streak of consciousness glowed weakly in infinite darkness, could he guess that there had been nothing.

So he guessed. He discovered time. As soon as his consciousness began to know its existence, he worked his way backwards. He needed a moment or an abyss of time to work his way back to his first memory, that very first spark. And notice that the memory had already faded.

Snapshots built his time. And then, slowly, his world.

He still was everything. He could remember seeing and hearing, but he didn't see or hear anything. This is hell, he thought; the first words he would remember from this existence. The words felt familiar and he tasted them, repeated them. This is hell.

No, another part of him said, this is heaven.

Just a few moments, or an eternity, had passed before he split up and began arguing with himself. So this isn't heaven, he thought, nor is it hell; because now I'm thinking, and I'm doing this in some kind of time.

He blinked several times. This felt almost as usual. Not quite but almost.

There was nothing to see.

I am everything, he thought. I am unborn. A baby in the womb, floating in amniotic fluid, not knowing anything of a world outside.

A world outside. The words gave him inner pictures, strange visions appearing and fading. Two smiling eyes. An enormous wall, white in merciless sunshine, warm and somehow a part of himself. He felt safe by the wall. And then there was an immense darkness where lights slowly moved.

He thought: Stars. There are stars in the outside world.

And I have a home. But not here.

Memories or dreams came and left. At some time he decided that he knew his name.

He was Jack.

The name brought new pictures. He supposed that they were of himself. His hands wanted to move up and feel his cheeks, his chin and forehead, to find out if his face agreed with the pictures.

He couldn't find his hands. They were somewhere out there, in the darkness between the stars, but he didn't know where.

He closed his eyes again and one of the burning dots grew. The light wasn't a star. Brown and reddish lines intertwined as it closed in.

Shylock, he thought. The light is a planet and it's named Shylock.

And I'm going there.

He thought it over one more time. He was a human being and his name was Jack. He had eyes that could blink but that didn't see anything when they were open. Not far from his eyes, he had ears.

The smiling face appeared again. Somehow exasperated, he pushed it away. It disturbed him. He didn't want to see it.

His own face was more coarse. Male, some part of his new consciousness whispered. He tried to remember what the other face was, if his own was male, but found no word.

Once again, he remembered that he had hands. And feet, his mind whispered. And legs.

And even further off, there was the red and brown planet named Shylock.

New snapshots came. He saw his feet and legs extending among the stars, lit by something that seemed to be on his left side. If there was a left, he knew, there had to be a right. His legs formed immense arcs, shimmering in the light. Like rainbows, he thought, but couldn't remember what that word meant. At the far end of the arcs he could make out the feet, almost invisible at this range. His feet were a pale yellow in this light and had a kind of buds that his mind called toes.

His toes felt the dirt of the planet Shylock. It was damp and cool. His feet tried to dig down into it but failed.

Once again, he wondered if this was hell.

His consciousness protested. And then the world exploded with light.

The light was followed by sound. A subdued murmur, something that he recognized as voices. Quietly speaking, softly. Several different.

One of the voices spoke so close that he flinched.

"Jack," the voice said. "Good morning, Jack."

Something grabbed him and he felt himself moving. Head, arms and chest quickly cooled as fluid trickled down.

Out of reflex, he tried to say "Good morning," but there was no sound. Instead, he vomited great amounts of fluid. This splashed down into more fluid, still covering his lower body and legs. Vomiting made his stomach turn and he threw up again. He gasped for air, realized that he hadn't breathed for seventy-three years, and in that moment he suddenly remembered everything.

Jack was at the table with the others. He recognized most of them, although they didn't look quite as they had seventy-three years ago. Everybody was thinner now, gaunt.

The planet Shylock had a gravity one and a half times that of Earth. The colonists had needed new bodies.

Jack recognized his friends but yet not. There was Veen, there was Peter, Sara and Borodin. Veen, who had been unusually old while they trained, probably over sixty. Peter and Sara, who looked like siblings but were a couple, and who still were somewhere around thirty, the most common age.

And little Borodin, living in a fifteen-year-old body.

Now Jack was nineteen. He didn't recognize his own body either. But he knew this was as it should be.

It would feel like breaking in new shoes. It always did.

"The trip went according to plan," said Borodin, the navigator. He still had his sharp blue eyes; in his fifteen-year-old face, they were even more striking. He smiled briefly. "All the ships are where they should be and no one seems to be the worse for wear by stasis."

"How long?" asked Sara.

Borodin shrugged. "About a day to orbit. A few hours more for check-ups and then we'll separate the ships."

"It's exciting," Sara said. "Shylock ..."

"Or Keenan c," Peter said quickly. "Thirty-two light-years from Earth, larger mass than our home planet, drier."

"But who cares." Sara's voice was dreamy. "Facts are uninteresting. I want to walk on the ground. Feel the gravity in my body."

Jack remembered the feeling of his toes on cold ground. He said, "What we have, now, here in the ship." An enormous yawn surprised him, made him cough up more synthetic amniotic fluid, and he realized both that he was dizzy and that his words were garbled. "Here in the ship," he tried again, "is this 1.46 gravity?"

"Yes," Borodin said. "We've had this since our bodies were fully grown a few months ago. And by the way, they all work perfectly."

Veen spoke for the first time. Dark eyes, dark hair, and Jack also seemed to remember dark thoughts. "Mine feels ... strange."

"Mine too," Sara and Peter said unanimously.

"Jack?" Borodin watched him.

"Sure. But that's normal, right?"

"Yes." Borodin held up his hand, bent and straightened his fingers, watched them move. Sara and Peter followed suit.

I'm almost two hundred years old, Jack thought. Two hundred and sixty-four years have passed since I was first born. Including seventy-three years in stasis.

Veen was the oldest among them. Not just because he had chosen to live in a sixty-year-old body on Earth, but because that body was his eighteenth. He hadn't said anything else about his age. But averaging thirty years in each body, this might mean more than five hundred years.

Jack wondered if Veen had brought all his stored memories. To Jack himself, this wasn't much of a problem. When he decided to leave he had cleared out all his dreary years, had left them at home in two backups, one in northern Finland and the other in Hawaii.

The memories he carried now were from his childhood, which he had never cared very much about; a few successful years as an adult, stuff that the psychologists said was good to carry with him; and his training, six months with Borodin, Veen and the others.

The rest of his memories were still on Earth, in cloned copies of his own brain tissue, dreamlessly waiting in nourishing fluid and oxygen. At least the experts said that they were dreamless, that the parts of the brain copied for storage had no consciousness.

Sometimes Jack thought that the experts were wrong. That his copied memories all along had had, or that they somehow had created, a consciousness. A mind that was stuck in its memories, reliving them over and over again.

A streak of light, he thought, like when I awoke from stasis. The hope of a streak of light. And the slowly growing horror that the streak will never come. Lying helplessly tangled in never-ending tendrils of your own memories. Waiting for something that you may never see.

He comforted himself by remembering that he hadn't experienced anything like that during the trip.

At least not that he could remember. And he couldn't know what was happening in his stored memories.

Bodies were simple. Bodies were grown from the owner's genetic make-up, sometimes modified, and reached adulthood in twelve to fifteen years. It did happen that people wanted to experience a childhood in their new bodies. Of course, sometimes bodies slept, like Jack and his friends had done now: their bodies had been grown for almost two decades and then kept sleeping.

When they only had a few weeks left to go, the ship's biological computer inoculated memories and higher brain functions into the bodies. And about a day before the ships arrived, the humans woke, confused and uncertain in their new bodies.

The ship itself was also made from biological material, quite often human. The outer hull was grown from Jack's own tooth enamel.

He lay on his little bed, the one that had recently been an aquarium with a body in stasis, thinking about this. His finger clumsily moved towards his mouth and had to poke at his upper lip to get in.

His tooth enamel was hard and wet. Jack's finger slid along it in wonder. Two feet from him was hard vacuum.

His teeth were in his mouth. His mouth was a part of himself. And he himself was contained in his own teeth.

He imagined shooting pains in his teeth, the enamel cracking. The vacuum of space would feel icy cold. Those few seconds before his blood boiled and his body slowly ruptured.

§

Among his obligatory memories, the common schooling that everybody carried, Jack had pictures of old-age technology. The time before multis.

That technology was as hard and unrelenting as the metal it was made of. It had passed with its age. Jack remembered holos of empires crumbling, and of cathedrals and bank buildings of glass and steel blowing up, rusting or being dismantled. But there was a limit to how much steel could be recycled. And when the oil ran out, oil and gas and all other fossilized hydrocarbons that had been burned as fuel as long as the shales were there, the age of steel also ended.

And then the multis came.

They had appeared simultaneously in many places. No one was sure where they came from. The accepted version was that they were from parallel worlds and had the power of technology to travel in the multiverse, the almost infinite number of universes existing alongside each other. That had given them the name "multis."

Multis were a little larger than humans, about seven feet tall, and seemed to have a few arms and legs. Not much else was known about them, since they didn't seem to have exact boundaries in space. They seemed to have some kind of kernel, but around this, they were layers of flowing gases or fluids. Not even high-speed cameras could show exactly where a multi ended and its surroundings began.

Multis were called "it," since nobody had been able to tell if they had sexes.

Neither did anyone know the number of possible universes. This difficulty was akin to the difficulty of defining a multi – exactly how large was the universe, and how long would it exist? Writers speculated in numbers like a googol: the number 1 followed by a hundred zeroes. But nobody knew for sure.

§

Multis had no clearly discernable mouth and, seemingly, no other organs for speech. They communicated by pictures. Series of pictures or dreams, as fluid and hard to interpret as themselves. Somehow, they also seemed to be able to read the minds of humans. When humans met a multi, they often experienced some kind of picture or vague idea in their mind. The humans automatically tried to interpret the picture; and the multi sending the picture didn't give up, no matter how many strange interpretations the humans made, but kept sending the picture over and over again, sometimes just repeating it and sometimes slowly changing it, until the humans at last understood its meaning.

The picture or dream could often be a solution to a problem. A blueprint for a biological machine; a suggestion of a certain modification of DNA; an explanation of what this modification could accomplish.

From multis, humans had received the ability to change biological material.

DNA technology could be as tough as modified tooth enamel.

Or as soft as lips and cheeks.

Landfall in seven hours. The ship did most of the work by itself, helped by Borodin and his matter-of-fact analyses. Still, Jack, Veen, Sara and Peter sat in the ship's single common room, following what happened. There was nothing to do, the small bunks were getting claustrophobic, and by now they were slowly getting accustomed to their new bodies.

A screen showed arid and waste ground.

"Red sand," Borodin said.

"Iron," Sara immediately said, and once again Jack could feel Peter's irritation. Something wasn't right between the two.

"Doesn't have to be iron," Veen said softly. "It could be some other mineral, or even some atmospheric refraction. There were arguments about Mars for years."

"So who was right?" Peter said. He was redheaded and pale. Genes from the polar circle, probably further east than Jack's Swedish ones. Skin almost transparent.

"Can't remember." Veen's smile was apologetic. Jack wondered if he had entered the conversation just to show that he didn't know. That it wasn't necessary to be perfect.

A few moments of silence. Sara smiled uncertainly at Peter but he looked down, avoiding her gaze.

Red wastelands slid by below them.

"And for this, I sold my soul," Jack said.

"You don't have a soul," Peter said immediately. "You only have innumerable manifestations in the multiverse."

Jack shrugged. "Whatever."

"We all sold our souls," Veen said.

Jack raised his palms. His hands were already responding better. His muscles were stronger than what he was accustomed to. At first, it had felt like lifting a cup that you believe to be full but that turns out empty. Now he could almost control his hands as he was used to. "It's only an expression," he said, "don't put too much in it."

"We sold our souls," Veen repeated without looking away from the screen. "They're stored on Earth and in our ships. Anyone can get to them."

Nobody answered.

Jack thought: What a strange thing to say.

Landing was a critical moment and an hour before entering the atmosphere, the ship split up into five. The twenty-nine other ships did the same. If anything went wrong, better that just one person died in their ship than all five.

Jack was alone with himself and his thoughts. He lay in his narrow tub again, covered up to his neck in water, since fluid was an excellent protection against shocks.

He had a needle in his arm, grown from Borodin's bone tissue. The colorless fluid in the thin tube was melatonin based and would calm him, possibly even make him sleep, until they were on the planet.

He didn't have to do anything at all during landing. Parts of Borodin's cloned brain, including Borodin's knowledge and calm, took care of everything.

Jack leaned his head against the lip-soft pillow behind his head and closed his eyes. The melatonin slowly did its work.

Once again he was everybody and everything, and thus nothing. From all directions at once he could see toothy smiles flash against dark skies as the atmosphere heated the ships' enamel. Soon, he saw the ships go out and disappear as they cooled again.

His eyes were still closed. Rich imagination, he thought, my imagination is unbelievably rich. Within himself he saw the landed ships being dragged together to larger huts, huts for two or six or eight persons, and parts designed to grow together beginning to sprout.

He tried to move his arms in the water but couldn't.

He was indistinct, blurred, like a multi, floating between the universe of air and of water, between his old world and his new.

2

Shylock's days were a little shorter than Earth's, just twenty-one hours. The days passed quickly. The planet had no moon and the nights were darker than Veen's eyes.

The village of huts slowly grew together. The one hundred and fifty ships had landed in two concentric circles and were already extending tendrils towards each other. At the same time, roots dug into the dirt, sucking up nutrients and minerals needed for growing.

With time, the slowly growing buildings would form two circles of living space, most of them connected but some standing by themselves, for people who wanted to be alone.

There was no higher animal life on the planet, but there were insects and plants: ferns, bushes and rough grass. The insects and plants differed from Earth's but were basically created from the same DNA.

This was true for every planet colonized thus far. Either the building materials of life were universal, or somebody had spread them. Multis or somebody else.

During the short nights, Jack dreamed of growing plants and trees. He longed to see Earth's plants break through the miserly earth.

He would have to wait. For now, he had to make do with the strange scepters and formations growing in his own brain.

After about a week, everybody had found their routines. Most of the colonists lived in the ships they had traveled in. Since the trip subjectively only had lasted a couple of days, all relations were the same as when it began.

Jack's hut was next to Borodin's. Veen lived on Borodin's other side and at Jack's other side were Peter and Sara; Peter's hut was closest to Jack's and was usually empty, since Peter and Sara slept together.

Jack wondered how the two were doing. He knew that the bodies they had had on Earth weren't their first, but he had no idea how many bodies they each had had before, or how long they had inhabited them. In a way, they seemed very young. Young and in love, but with quite a few problems left to solve.

But then, who didn't have problems? He himself had used up three or four bodies during his two hundred years. Still, he felt immature, unfinished.

A child in his fifth body.

Veen stayed gloomy. Nobody knew why, but Jack heard Sara and Peter talk about it. One day, Borodin also hinted at Veen's mood.

"I don't know," Jack said. "Maybe it's just the way he is."

"He should have modified. Gotten rid of it."

"It's his choice."

"Doesn't it bother you?"

"No," Jack said. "He is who he is."

A third of a mile away was the brownish sea, most often with white geese and under ragged clouds that chased each other. The beach was rocky and forbidding.

Beyond the beach was tundra. Moss and lichen, and the budding experimental farms with Earth's plants.

At the horizon: jagged mountains below black clouds. And a red-brown sky.

They worked with genetically modified plants – the flowers and trees that Jack still dreamed of, but mostly crops, kinds of corn and cereal that were hybrids of oats and rye, of wheat and sesame. In time, the cold winds would be slowed down by trees and bushes, and the plan was that temperatures would slowly rise. But for now it was cold.

They worked in teams of ten, two ships, paired up from the inner and outer circles. The work was heavy. Other colony planets used modified draft animals that sometimes were more like machines, but Shylock's colonists had chosen to go with fewer ships; in time, the colonists would create modified animals, but not yet. Jack blew on his cold fingers and filled his seed sack again.

The five from the outer circle he only knew by name. They seemed to be from the Pacific: Keawe and Kokua, Haole, Liliua, Kamakaeha. Keawe was the one showing most of his original genes, with brown skin and, at least in his Earth body, a tendency to fat. Liliua was beautiful.

The colonists' muscles had been developed by biological machines in the ships, up to the day when their memories were transferred to their brains and they left stasis.

The bodies were mostly ordinary nineteen-year-olds, though modified for Shylock's gravity. They were also modified to be attracted to one another, slender and tiny as they were, and hormones played.

"You are beautiful," Jack said to Liliua while they went another lap. Their arms moved in rhythm: reaching down into the seed sack, grabbing a handful, spreading it over the newly turned dirt.

"Thanks," she said. Her smile was a little uncertain. "And you are ...?"

"I'm beautiful too," he immediately said.

She smiled again. "No, I mean, what's your name?"

"Oh, sorry. I'm Jack."

"Jack. I'm Liliua. But everybody calls me Liya."

"Liya. Hi."

"Hello."

They exchanged more tentative phrases before his sack was empty and he left her to fill it again. He couldn't keep from looking at her during the brown afternoon.

His mind, his soul, as some people would say, was two hundred years old. He was quite aware of how relationships grew and withered.

Still, he wanted her. The hormones in his nineteen-year-old body controlled his two centuries old mind.

Other days they went looking for minerals and nutrients. DNA was a beautiful machine, the perfect nano-machine that humanity had wanted to emulate before everything changed, and could create a human being, an elephant, an enamel ship or a scorpion. But minerals were necessary. A few of the colonists were specially trained to find them – Veen and Borodin and Liliua, of the group working with Jack. Twice a week they went to the sharp mountains and didn't come home until late at night, tired and dejected.

"It's worse than we thought," Veen said one night. "Silicates and sulfates abound, but there are almost no phosphates."

"Meaning?" Jack said. He should have known but hadn't really cared for his studies. Liliua, Liya, passed on her way to her own circle, her head also hanging. Jack's hormones immediately urged him to comfort her. He managed to stop the impulse.

"Phosphates are important for bone tissue and teeth," Veen said as Liya disappeared.

"Oh."

A couple of days later, Liya came running back to the village. She called out at a distance, hair streaming in the wind.

"Phosphates! Phosphates!"

There was a party.

The colony had no single leader, but a council that was chosen every fiftieth day. Jack knew nobody in the present council. It was obvious that they had planned. They had managed to cultivate ganja, brew beer and distil vodka for the party.

A hundred and fifty people were gathered in the open space within the circles. They stood or sat around in groups, talking and laughing. A few of them played musical instruments, singing old songs that Jack could remember from his real childhood, and others joined in.

Louder and louder as the vodka sank in its bottles.

Hormones did their work. The singing gradually died as couples or groups disappeared into huts.

Jack's eyes sought Liya. He didn't see her.

He wondered what she was doing.

He had a hard time sleeping that night. Ganja hadn't been common where he grew up. As an adult, he'd tried it a few times but never really understood its charm. Two times he just grew tired and the third he'd been sick and vomited.

Instead of ganja he kept to vodka, the liquor most common in northern Sweden when he came of age, still dominating in its belt from Iceland to Siberia. Tonight, he'd been a little too faithful to his vodka, and when he lay down on his bed and clumsily covered himself with the soft blanket, he was reminded of this.

I could have found her, he thought. Talked to her.

The impulse had been in his young body. But his old soul stopped him from following it. Something in her eyes, her way of moving, told him that her consciousness was a lot younger than his.

Things could easily go wrong.

He could see it happen: himself talking to Liya, her eyes uncertain. And then, when somebody else with a nineteen-year-old body, moving in that loose way that showed that his soul wasn't much older, came up to her, they lit up. The other guy sat down – no, Jack changed this – no, Liya rose and followed him.

He felt the little hut spin and firmly put one foot on the floor. For a moment, he wondered how many people had tried to avoid vomiting in this way. During how many thousands of years.

He saw an unbroken chain, thousands of years long, of feet put on floors to keep their owners from throwing up.

This thought was enough and he ran out.

The party continued. A few singers refused to give up, their voices billowing and surging. Jack was leaned over behind his hut, unprotected from the cold wind, while the minerals in his stomach fertilized the ground.

He thought he was done and inhaled sharply. But new spasms came.

Nineteen years old, he thought. Never drank before.

I should have known.

"How are you?"

Jack came out of it. He blinked in surprise and remembered the feeling. Waking from nothing and slowly returning to the world.

"Are you okay?"

Jack got to his knees. He quickly glanced at the pool he had made on the ground. Then at his clothes.

At least, he hadn't slept in the pool.

"What?" he said, voice thick.

"Are you sick?"

Of course it was Liya. She must have seen him from her own hut, fifteen yards away.

He gaped at her, fish-eyed.

"V-vodka," he got out. The word itself gave him more spasms. But there was nothing left to throw up.

"You can't lie here," she said. "Come," and she reached out with her hand. He thankfully took it.

"It's o-okay," he said when he'd found parts of his balance. "Just a little too much to drink."

"I'm sorry." She smiled. "But it was self-inflicted."

Her eyes were lovely. Large and widely spaced. He could drown in those eyes.

But he didn't know what to say to her.

A little later, he was in his bed again. There were no more spasms and he slept, dreaming of Liya's eyes.

She was dark. Her skin was quite light but her hair was very dark. She was almost exactly his height and had the same elongated body.

Still so beautiful.

Her eyes were blue. He didn't know if this was Hawaiian or if she had modified them.

The colonists struggled on. After the first party, social life slowly grew. There were no more parties for a while, since the first one had used up almost all the vodka and ganja. Jack wasn't disturbed by this. He could still feel that taste in his mouth.

It was the first time this body had thrown up from alcohol.

And, he thought, it's still a virgin. I'm not. But my body is.

§

Instead of lavish parties, the colonists enjoyed themselves with smaller gatherings. Many of them had brought libraries of holos and virtuals from Earth. The difference was crucial: a holo you watched from outside; in a virtual, you yourself were the main character.

There were historic dramas, documentaries, old plays and flat-films. The prudent watched harmless holos but before long, there were rumors of colonists carrying virtuals of serial killers and other weirdness thirty-two light-years from their home planet.

"Phew," Liya said one day when they met in the fields. The short summer had begun and it was possible to be outside without a parka. They were digging irrigation ditches. "You think it's for real?"

Jack shook his head. "No. It can't be."

"Why?" She looked pleading. Let me have my hope, her eyes said.

"Nobody has been able to transpose memories from one person to another. Don't worry, it's fake. Somebody wrote a script and somebody recorded and programmed something that feels like real emotions and experiences."

"Are you sure?"

He smiled at her. "Absolutely."

She smiled back.

"It's funny," she said a while later. "The difference between holos and virtuals, I mean."

"How?"

Liya gesturing, grasping for words. "You know. You are *in* virtuals but not in holos."

Jack stopped digging for a moment. "Well," he said, "that's sort of the idea."

"I know. But when you *think* about it. We saw this holo about Genghis the Second a couple of nights ago ..."

You and who else? a little voice inside Jack asked. Outwardly, he just nodded.

"The difference between seeing and experiencing," Liya said. She let her shovel fall and sat on reddish earth. Jack joined her. Cold seeped in through his pants.

"We saw half of the holo until somebody suggested we should experience the rest of it virtually." She watched Jack. "Have you seen it?"

He shook his head. "I know about Genghis the Second."

"Yes. Maybe you were alive then?" She immediately blushed. "Sorry, I'm sorry, I didn't mean –"

"No problem. It's four hundred and fifty years ago and no, I wasn't born then. But I did go to school. He conquered Central Asia and half of Europe."

"Right." She nodded, relieved. "Anyway, we went to the virtual right when he entered Europe."

"And?"

Her hands worked the air as if they were trying to grab something. "Genghis wasn't a, how to put it, a very good person. All that killing."

"Yeah." He remembered unpleasant scenes from holos.

"But then, when you joined him in the virtual, you ... you *understood* him, somehow. You know what I mean?" Her eyes pleaded again.

"You know why he did what he did."

"Yes. All that killing. Even I could grasp his motives."

"It's hard to hate anybody that you've seen from inside. Even if it's just a construction."

"Suppose you could trade memories. For real."

Jack shook his head.

"But you can't. That would be telepathy. It was tried and people died."

The huts slowly grew to houses. During the height of the summer Jack could enter his upper floor for the first time, although he had to stoop. He could see out through growing windows, all the way to the stormy sea.

He could see Liya's hut.

That night he dreamed of a mouth full of teeth. The teeth slowly grew, starting out as small white swellings in gums, to fully-grown frontals and molars. When he watched closer, he could see small hatches in the teeth. Strange little creatures scurried up and down, chasing each other in what could be war or love.

He woke and thought, I have to curb my imagination.

Benoit the Belgian called a meeting at the end of summer

"I'll get straight to the point," he said. He was even thinner than most, and not very tall, but he had a natural authority and people would have listened to him even if he hadn't been in the council.

They were gathered inside the circles again. But the houses were higher now and everybody knew each other better.

"The crops will be poorer than we hoped," Benoit said after a short pause. "Quite a lot poorer."

Haole raised a slim hand.

"Well, we knew that?"

"Right," Benoit said. "We knew. But we couldn't foresee how bad it really is. We still lack some minerals and a large part of the harvest will be more or less worthless. If we only have that to eat during winter, we'll suffer deficiency diseases."

"We brought stores," somebody in the circles closest to Benoit called out.

"True," the Belgian said. "We did. But it wouldn't be smart to use them this early. We might have crises when we need reserves."

"So what do you suggest?"

"The *council* suggests," Benoit said, stressing the second word, "that we try to grow another crop. It won't be easy, it will be very late in summer, maybe fall, before we can harvest. And we have to work very hard to find more fertilizing minerals." He paused again. "This goes for everybody. No exceptions."

"You too?" the anonymous voice called.

"Yes," Benoit said. "Me too."

A few voices protested but everybody realized the seriousness of their situation. Early next morning, groups walked towards the mountains.

The work was heavy, heavier than digging ditches. The pickaxe chafed his hands. He worked stooped, looking for the special glitter that Haole had described.

Jack struggled on, stubborn and sweaty.

Within, he dreamed of Liya.

3

"It's better than Earth, anyway," Sara said.

The second harvest was in, meaning that they would make it through the winter with a fine margin. There wasn't much left over to make ganja and alcohol, but most of the colonists seemed to have accepted that.

They were still searching for minerals. Autumn had come, slow and cold. There was still a short month left until the equinox.

"Well, I'm not so sure," Peter said.

There was still something strange about the two. Sara said something, most often something positive, and Peter immediately contradicted her. After a couple of lines, Sara was silent, and Peter unfailingly looked disappointed.

"We can create our own world here," Sara tried. "Our own society."

"All societies become alike in the end. An upper class emerges, controlling power and money."

Sara turned away, hacking at the ground. Jack wanted to say something but he didn't know what.

Everybody felt the severe climate and the meager resources.

"Nobody knows how many colonies have made it," Peter said.

They were lunching in lee of a sharp cliff. Below the cliff, strange plants had turned the ground to crumbly dirt.

"Not writing home doesn't mean they're dead," Veen pointed out. "Nobody expects the fish people of Ypsilon Andromedae b to write home every week. Or the fliers of Mu Arae."

"And if they had," Keawe said, "their messages might have been gibberish to Earth people. Fish people or bird people probably don't think like us any more. And many groups left just because they didn't like Earth and wanted to get away."

"Like us," Keawe noted.

"But there's a difference." Peter immediately struck. "Soon, Earth will become crowded again, and who wants to live at the equator and spend all their time with sun and bathing and virtuals?" Sara wanted to say something but he interrupted her. "And I was so tired of that New Awakening. The born-again Christianity. Soon, they'll end up like last time, with religious wars."

"Well, there aren't that many other religions to fight," Veen said. "Most areas where Islam and Judaism were strong melted to glass during the upheavals."

"And by the way, much in those wars wasn't really about religion." Sara spoke quickly, before anybody else cut in. "Religions were just a pretext. It was all about resources."

Jack listened. He was interested in what was said, as well as worried for Sara. She seemed to feel strongly about what she said, but he also felt that she was holding back, no doubt to avoid irritating Peter. Still, Peter seemed to be upset when Sara kept talking about newly Awaked people who left their bodies for the last time to die for real.

"Christians have been morons throughout the ages," Peter said. "What you're saying is equal to those idiots who want to keep living on Earth because other copies of them, versions in other universes, already are blessed. Or those who imagine that there is one single paradise for all universes and that that's where people finally get whole. Or those who speculate about how many copies of God there are in the multiverse." He shook his head. "Idiots. Complete idiots."

Sara looked down at the ground.

Jack took heart.

"Don't mind him," he said later in the afternoon, during a break when he and Sara were alone.

"Peter?" Her face was spiteful.

Jack nodded. "He doesn't mean anything bad."

Spite again. "And what's that to you?"

"Nothing." He shrugged, tried to explain. "I've just noticed that he always contradicts you."

"Which is none of your business."

He nodded again. Caught her eye. "I'm sorry."

Sara immediately softened. "No matter," she said.

"No, you're right. I shouldn't pry."

"You think everybody feels like you?"

"I have no idea," he said. "I just thought –" He didn't know how to continue.

She stood. The wind tugged at her hair as she looked up to the sky. Gray-brown clouds scudded from the sky and in over the jagged mountains.

"Sometimes it's terrible," she said. "Sometimes I think I ought to leave him. That's why I said those things about Earth before." She looked Jack in the eye, a glance telling him that she was sharing a secret. "On Earth, I may have found somebody else."

"Can't you do that here? There are plenty of –"

"Who? Veen who's even worse than Peter? Borodin, who only lives for his formulas?"

He hesitated. "The Hawaiians," he said. "Or –"

"Or you?" she interrupted, although he hadn't been thinking of himself at all. Her voice softened again. "I wouldn't have been uninterested," she said, "I wouldn't have been uninterested in you. And several other women have been talking about you. Not just me. But everybody knows you and Liya are going to end up together."

Strange feelings rose in him.

"I didn't know that," he said.

"No. Of course not. You're a man. But everybody else ..."

The talk with Sara made him cautious. He had had no idea that the women of the colony saw him in that way – he'd never guessed that he could have been interesting to them, or that they might have seen anything happening between him and Liya.

I've been too interested, he thought. The classical mistake: wanting her so much, I've kept back. And yet, they've seen it.

I have to be careful with the others. Especially Sara.

He didn't want to irritate Peter.

As autumn darkened, he became more attentive. He noted glances, fragments of conversation, shy smiles.

He saw relationships grow and crumble.

But he didn't dare to tell Liya how he felt.

He wondered why.

At equinox, the new council chairman, a blond and unusually broad American named Taylor, informed the colonists that food would be rationed. His words were met with silence. Everybody wanted to protest, but nobody had a better idea.

Like everybody else, Jack spent more time worrying about the colony's future than thinking about sex and other pleasures. He noticed the silence from the latest group meeting dragging out for days.

There was no risk for famine. If worst came to worst they could modify the still growing huts, now rather houses, back to ships again. Leave their bodies here and travel back. Or send a radio message, reaching Earth in thirty-two years instead of seventy-three, and have a new body grown there.

§

Nobody wanted to do that. Returning to Earth would feel like failure. Jack worked hard, ate his meager rations and drank water when his stomach protested.

Things had to get better.

One evening he came home, exhausted and sweaty after spending a day searching for minerals, and met a multi.

This was the first time he saw a multi on Shylock and he was surprised.

"Hi," he said. Since multis communicated by mental pictures, a kind of telepathy that still was impossible to humans, the easiest way was to simply use your own language. The theory was that multis read the pictures in your own brain, before they were expressed in language, and then answered in an intelligible way – at least most of the time. Although you might have to ponder the blurry pictures for a while.

The multi sent a picture that Jack interpreted as a warm welcome. Jack wondered if he'd seen this multi before. The creatures were impossible to tell apart.

However, this one seemed larger than the ones Jack had seen before. Jack studied the multi, and in a few moments he got a picture of his old body standing next to his new. His new body was almost a head shorter than the old one and of course a lot thinner.

The multi projected himself next to Jack and Jack remembered what he knew but seldom had thought about since he came here: that the colonists' bodies weren't only differently proportioned but also smaller. This was economical in many contexts, from room in the ships to food.

The fuzzy cloud that was the multi didn't send any more pictures.

"What are you doing here?" Jack said in a few moments. The multi sent back a picture of a boy playing next to a stream, the mother watching over him.

"Babysitter?" Jack said.

He saw a flickering image of starving people.

"Is it that bad?"

But the multi disappeared without further pictures.

"Did anybody see a multi since we came here?" Jack asked the next day. Nobody said yes.

Jack thought quite a lot about the short meeting. Multis always were unpredictable. Nobody knew how they traveled through space or between universes. Also, their communications were not always easily understood, and they had a disturbing habit of seldom confirming when you asked if you'd understood them correctly. Notwithstanding, Jack thought that he'd interpreted the image of the child and mother correctly – the colony, or at least Jack, was in danger, and the multi was watching over them.

The multi's presence should have been a comfort. But on the contrary, it seemed to make Jack worried.

Knowing you were in danger was troublesome.

As winter closed in, it became impossible to gather everybody in the same place: the weather was too cold and there was no indoor space large enough. An evening a few weeks after the equinox, some of the neighbors gathered in Keawe's hut. Not everybody was present – Haole had something else to do, Borodin was immersed in his formulas, Veen had just failed to appear – but the remaining seven still had to crowd each other. Jack ended up next to Liya.

His conversation with Sara a few weeks ago still made him tense. To him, it felt as if most of the people in the room were glancing at him and Liya. He was certain when he met Sara's glance and she quickly raised her brows.

He didn't know what he might say to Liya. Just that he was attracted to her.

Liya tried to solve his problem.

"Tell me about yourself," she said.

"Me?" he said stupidly.

"Who else? That table?"

"Well ..." He tried to think but didn't find anything interesting to say.

"I know quite a lot about everybody else here," Liya said, "by now. But not about you. You always keep to yourself and seldom say anything. The only thing I know is that you're a genius with DNA."

He looked into her large eyes and wished that he'd been able to let loose the tidal wave churning in his frontal lobes. He just didn't dare. It was impossible to know how she would react and he didn't want to be the talk of the colonists.

"Well then," he said, gearing up. "Born in northern Sweden, about two hundred years before we left."

"Northern Sweden?" she said. "Ice and snow? Polar bears?"

He made a so-so gesture with his hand. "Ice and snow, definitely. During winters. Polar bears ... I think maybe a couple were seen just before we left, but they've been scarce after the upheavals."

"Didn't the Nature Council create new ones?"

"True." When she mentioned this, he wondered why he'd not kept that memory. "They must have done, or else we wouldn't have and polar bears at all by now."

"If they even exist by now," she said. She was holding a glass of water but seemed to wish it had been something else. "Seventy-three years ... we don't even know if the planet is still there."

"No. But what about you?"

"Me?" She echoed his own answer earlier.

He thought she blushed just a little. And Sara was looking at them again.

"Where are you from? Who are you?"

"Hawaii. But you knew that, right? The big island. Born three hundred years ago, this is my sixth body, had five on Earth." She seemed more used to talking about herself than he. "I was a New Christian for a time but that gave me nothing. I had a nice life materially, like everybody in the Pacific, but nothing that gave me a rush. I wanted to live more, see other things."

"And you chose Shylock?"

"Well, it's quite different from Hawaii."

Their conversation flowed more freely, but the more they talked, the more uneasy Jack felt. Everybody seemed to be staring at him. When Keawe and Kokua stood and left together, they were applauded. Jack excused himself and left.

He cursed himself even before he was home. Well, why should it matter? he thought. Let them talk.

Or, he realized, maybe I don't want to. In spite of those eyes.

Still, he felt himself being attracted to her.

He cursed himself again.

Instead, he thought about multis. He'd met them a few times before going to Shylock. Nobody knew why they contacted humans. All encounters seemed to be random. Or maybe the encounters were part of an unknown agenda. Something that no human being could understand.

Jack was irritated that he couldn't remember more about multis. He knew that they'd taught him to modify DNA; even in his first body, he'd been able to cure diseases and create strange creatures that sometimes had been able to live, sometimes not.

He dreamed for a long time that night. The dream began with the miniature monsters he'd made as a young man; he saw them flap and wail, dying on the floor of his room or breaking themselves against walls. He remembered a short moment of consciousness in the middle of the dream when he'd wondered if monsters always had looked the same. Lizards and demons with jagged wings and cruel faces.

The dream slid along and turned into vague longing. The next day he tried to find something in it that may have pointed to Liya; maybe large and enormous eyes; but there was nothing like that.

He wanted to return to the dream. There was some time before he had to go looking for minerals again. He closed his eyes and tried to sink. Downward through memories.

Just a vague longing. Like a piece of music remembered after many years, an undefined sadness.

4

The winter was warmer than they'd predicted. Snow covered the ground for a few weeks around the winter solstice, but the ground never froze. Beneath the houses, roots kept sending tendrils further out and the houses still grew, although more slowly.

It was very dark. Modified lantern eye fishes and glowing plants supplied most of the colony's light, but the outside lamp trees hadn't grown yet. During long winter nights, finding your way between the houses wasn't easy.

The colonists worked hard during daylight hours. At last, they had found a couple of rich deposits, close to the mountain range, where it was possible to mine ore that could be refined into different minerals.

It felt as if the colony was hibernating. Like the roots under their houses, the blood in the humans' veins seemed to flow slower, more sluggish. Heated arguments had given way to quiet admonitions; wild laughter was replaced by quiet smiles.

Jack stood in front of one of the biological refiners and seemed to feel his own heart slow, his breathing become more and more calm; finally, he felt the processes in his brain almost grinding to a halt. But it was just an illusion. Some kind of psychological reaction to the dark winter.

Although conversations were more silent, many things still happened under the surface. A couple of the women were pregnant and their midriffs grew in step with the days getting longer after midwinter. In the same way, the colonists gradually came to be a society. People found their roles, adjusted to these and to each other.

If the planet had been less stingy and inhospitable, life in the colony would have been idyllic.

Many long winter nights were filled with discussions. Jack learned a lot by listening to the colony's oldest members. Keawe had memories of how multis first appeared on Earth.

"I saw it on the net," he said. "Internet, the first world net. The electronic one. The first multi appeared some time right after the upheavals, in Europe somewhere, and the rumor spread like wildfire. Very few believed it. It was just another blanket to hide from reality in ... And Europe was so far away.

"But there were more rumors. More news on the net. And in time it happened in Hawaii, then it happened to somebody I knew, and finally it happened to me."

"What happened?" said a girl who sat on the floor and who seemed excited by the concepts of multis. Maybe she had never met one. "How did it happen?"

"I was sitting outside my house in the mountains, a house that I'd built myself after a tsunami wrecked the city of Honolulu, where I'd lived ... I was sitting watching the sea. Like my people had done for a thousand generations. And then there was something in the way, something that blocked my view. I squinted but that didn't help. I saw a shadow between me and the sea. The shadow grew darker. It never became a solid body with defined limits, but it seemed to thicken. Like white smoke turning to black smoke turning to fluid and then to jelly ..."

Keawe smiled at the memory. Kokua squeezed his hand.

"Did the multi talk, I mean, communicate with you?"

Keawe's smile became pensive. "Yes. It sent me a picture of an apple tree, losing its fruits and then falling, rotting on the ground. And a new tree growing where the apples had fallen. I didn't understand. But the multi sent the picture again before it disappeared, fading away in the sunlight.

"Two weeks later, my father died."

Jack left Keawe's house and began walking the short distance home. After a moment, he heard steps behind him.

He turned. It was Liya.

"What do you want?" he asked. He had meant it to sound friendly but he could hear his voice sounding almost aggressive.

Liya looked uncertain. "Well ... nothing ..."

"I'm sorry," Jack blurted in embarrassment, "I didn't mean to –"

And Liya, in the same moment, "I just wanted –"

Both fell silent. And began again, simultaneously:

"I didn't mean to –"

"It was so depressing –"

"Depressing?" Jack caught the word and the question escaped him before he had time to think. "What was depressing?"

Her fingers built invisible minarets. "The upheavals. Multis. Mankind on its knees ..."

"But you must have known before."

"Yes," she said, "yes, obviously I have. But it grabbed me tonight." She swallowed. "I felt so alone ... Thirty-two empty light-years ..." She talked faster. "... I realized we are just biological creatures who live and then die ... and all we have is closeness to somebody else ..."

She suddenly interrupted herself. Jack couldn't remember any time during his two hundred years when he had had a come-on this unequivocal.

They went to her house.

He looked up into her enormous eyes.

Her eyes grew ever darker as she came close to orgasm and just before she closed them and fell over him, they were quite black.

In the morning both of them were embarrassed, didn't know what to say. Jack felt the ancient male urge to run, escape from what had happened.

Ruled by biology, he thought. Spread your genes and run.

Liya smiled uncertainly when he left.

The snow had melted long ago and some days the air almost felt warm. During a couple of days they could even see the sun: an enormous red-brown mass, hovering at the horizon. Jack stood on the shore and saw the sky break down in fantastic colors.

For the first time, he thought, Shylock was beautiful.

Walking back from the sea, he had an idea.

"What we should try," he said to Borodin later in the afternoon, "is to care a little less about the original ecology here. We've been quite careful with Earth genes. I suggest that we graft a lot more of them here. That we modify and change the very platform for life here."

"That might entail a conflict between different strands. Viruses –"

Jack raised his hand, fingers spread. "I'm aware of the risks. But we have to try something. Soon."

Borodin's blue eyes pierced him.

Jack's idea couldn't have been totally useless, since Borodin called a meeting that same evening. Veen, Borodin and five other biological experts; one of them was Liya.

And Jack himself.

Jack summarized his idea in a couple of minutes and a wild discussion followed.

When the discussion was almost over, when the same arguments were repeated over and over again, Borodin raised his hand. His boy's face was serious.

"Am I getting this right? Leto, Chema, Niall, Sandra and Liya against? Jack, Veen and me for?"

Eight heads nodded in unison.

Borodin turned to Jack. "I'll give you one more chance to convince us."

Jack shook his head. He had a few arguments left, and somehow, he knew he was right – he wasn't an expert in ecology but his natural faculty for handling genes still made him certain. But he didn't want to argue against Liya.

Veen seemed dissatisfied.

They had a spring party, a party where it turned out that quite a few of them had discovered new methods for making alcohol and other chemical amusement aids. The air was still growing warmer, summer was coming and everybody was in a good mood.

Quite late in the evening, Jack rose and walked around the gathering. He hadn't seen Liya there.

He didn't know if he was jealous or if he just longed for her.

Agitated voices from another group, further out in the darkness, caught his interest. He walked over there. No Liya. Jack was about to leave when he heard something.

"But according to Gödel's theorem," said an unusually dark-skinned and not quite sober man whom Jack thought might be called Uche, "no system can be complete without containing contradictions. And since God is supposed to be almighty and all-knowing and all-good – all these of course are different variants of completeness – he or she or it must also contain self-contradictions. This might be the reason why there's evil: the Devil is a contradiction in God's being ..."

Angry voices from New Christians and their antagonists drowned out the rest of Uche's rant. Jack thought about all the temples created by humans, both as buildings and within themselves: temples of stone or of dreams. Somehow, this thought made him low-spirited.

He couldn't find her anywhere.

A few minutes of indecision. Singing and loud voices from the middle of the circles; quiet houses around them.

He knocked.

"Why didn't you come to the party?" he asked her afterwards.

"I didn't dare," Liya said. "I was afraid you'd be angry with me because I didn't support your idea at that meeting." She smiled faintly. "I thought you'd find me if you wanted to."

"Well, I did."

"Yes!"

They found each other again. They made love two more times that night and again in the morning. The embarrassment and shyness were gone.

At last, Jack had admitted to himself that he wanted her.

§

They moved in together, which simply meant carrying a few possessions from one little house to the other. Jack chose to live at Liya's place only for the silly reason that he wanted to get further away from Sara: he could imagine how she would look at him. Jack and Liya lived together and were seldom apart for more than a few minutes. In the daytime, they worked together; during nights they discovered each other until they slept from exhaustion; but after a couple of hours one of them would move, both would wake, and Liya's eyes slowly darkened again.

They got to know each other. Liya told him about her childhood in Hawaii. She had been born there about three hundred years ago and her first body had grown on the big island, in the mountains, not far from where Keawe had built his house a couple of hundred years earlier.

"I was so ugly as a child," she said into her pillow, "terribly horribly ugly."

"Not you." He caressed her back. Her skin was brown and soft.

"Yes, me. I was disgustingly ugly. I don't know if my parents never checked what I would be, or if something went wrong – anyway, I looked like a cross-eyed chimp." She suddenly looked at him, a quick glance. "You know, chimps?"

He knew.

"So I moved to Oahu and rebuilt myself as soon as I was of age and could afford it."

"You are very beautiful now. However you may have looked then."

"Thank you. But it's still in me. I've changed bodies five times now, and every time I've gotten rid of a lot of memories. But at some level, I don't know those terms, maybe in the subconscious ... in my subconscious I still have those feelings from when I was a kid. Somehow. People turning. Children laughing. Whispers. People with their hands over their mouths to hide smiles or laughter."

He caressed her. She lifted her head from the pillow.

"Don't leave me," she said.

He shook his head. "I will erase those hidden memories. I will hunt them down and destroy them. You and I, we can do anything. Together. Anything at all."

But that was only words. He knew this even while speaking them.

Somewhere, deep within himself, he knew that he yearned.

This yearning was what had made him suggest Earth DNA. Shylock could be beautiful. The planet could become more like Earth, flowers could be made to explode from beds of biological engineering, and the more Earth-like Shylock became, the more Jack would like it.

But Shylock wasn't Earth yet. Far from it.

And Jack yearned.

They had made love again, slowly and tenderly all the way to the final moments; Liya's eyes had turned to veritable black holes, singularities where no laws applied and from which nothing could escape.

"I never want to escape from you," she said afterwards. Wedged in his armpit.

"Why would you have to do that?"

"You had a dream last night."

He moved to see her eyes. Lighter now, penetrable. Open to him. But not quite peaceful.

"What?"

"I don't know," she said. "You were moving. Uneasy. Mumbling to yourself, incomprehensible words. Turning, going silent, breathing unevenly."

"Can't remember."

"Don't leave me."

A few days later Jack met Veen alone, outside the village. Veen was standing by himself, looking at the mountains, when Jack came up from behind.

"Hello," Jack said a few steps away; he didn't want startle Veen.

"Hi." Veen quickly looked over his shoulder and then resumed staring at the mountains.

"What are you looking for?"

Veen stared for another second before turning to Jack. "Solitude."

"Solitude?"

Veen relaxed. "Why did you come here? To Shylock?"

Jack thought. "Adventure?"

"Come on." Veen's smile was twisted. "Adventure? Thirty-two light-years and then this bleak tundra, that's your idea of adventure?"

"It is. So why did *you* come?"

Veen spat and studied his saliva turning the dry ground dark. "There we go, some more Earth DNA for Shylock's micro-organisms to have fun with." He suddenly turned to Jack. "I don't like people."

Jack didn't answer. Veen gestured.

"I don't like people, in general. During my centuries I have met some people that I could get along with, sure. Most often recluses like myself. Nice paradox: the only people you like are people who also want to be alone. But at the same time, this means that you'll mostly leave one another be – which makes you stand each other."

"I see."

"And somehow, I guess I'd hoped that this colony would have a lot of such people. That we would work in the days, each on his own, some distance from everybody else; and at night, everybody would lock themselves into their huts and leave each other be."

"But that didn't happen."

"No. It didn't. There are gatherings and parties and meetings and co-operation. And this society is quite smaller than anything I experienced at home. Which makes it harder to hide."

Jack wanted to answer but couldn't find anything to say.

"I want to go back home again," Veen said. "I was standing here thinking when you came. A hundred and fifty people on the planet and you can't even be alone to think for just a couple of minutes.

"You don't have to shout this from the rooftops. But if you hear anybody else who wants to go home, let me know. You need five huts, modified back, to make a ship.

"And five people."

Later, going home, Jack met a multi again. The fusiform creature slowly waved back and forth outside the outer circle of houses. Fibers and filaments seemed to emerge from the tall quill to immediately retract back into it again.

"Give me a picture," Jack said. "Show me how Liya and I are doing in a few years."

Jack waited. A shimmering image of Shylock's barren land seemed to appear before him. But something about the landscape had changed. Trees had grown, small and strangely regular black trees.

Jack strained to see. The hazy trees seemed familiar.

The picture momentarily stabilized.

"Dead?" Jack said.

What he had seen was a graveyard. And the multi refused to send more pictures.

Jack dreamed he was a multi. Like animals, the multi had no self-consciousness; he was everything, oceanic, filling the earth, existing everywhere as well as nowhere.

He realized that he was dreaming of a dream, the dream he had had when he woke on the ship, almost one short year ago.

His longing was unbearable.

Liya woke him with a kiss.

"What –" He was both in his dream and with Liya. For a moment, he didn't know what was real and what was a dream. Then the set pieces of the dream crumbled.

He answered her kiss and it turned to something else.

"Thanks," he said when he was breathing normally again.

"What were you dreaming?"

"Everything," he said. "It's hard to explain. I was everything. Everything and nothing."

"You are everything to me. I'm just saying."

"Likewise."

He fell asleep with his arm around her. During the last moments, he didn't know if he was hearing her breathing or his own.

The last thing he thought was that Veen was wrong. People were not unbearable. Jack and Liya had managed to find each other, even if both of them had trouble communicating. Shylock was a barren place but could change for the better.

Everything would get better.

5

Things advanced, if slowly. Some time during high summer – which meant temperatures of up to sixty degrees Fahrenheit and sunshine several days in a row – a group of Canadian colonists discovered a massive mountain with quite a lot of useful minerals. Also, the colony was coming into its second year, which made recycling possible: the meager harvests of last year, human waste, leftover food ...

Of course, there were many meager years before them. But it wasn't impossible that even their current bodies would see better times.

Their joy was subdued when the first colonist died: a woman from southern Europe who was crushed by falling rocks in the new mining field. Of course, she would live again, but no sooner than in seven or eight years, and even in that case she'd have to be a child for several years; also, she would lose almost all her memories of Shylock, since she hadn't updated her backups since their fortieth day on the planet.

They held a memorial while the DNA machinery was already dismantling her body. After the little ceremony, sorrow seemed to dissipate. The dead woman, Jemima, hadn't had many close friends on Shylock and was only missed by two or three people.

Veen was one. He was gloomy.

"She wanted to go back," he said to Jack while they went back from the summer-red sea. "I had two companions. One more and I could have asked you. But now I need two before I can do that."

"What makes you think I want to go back?" Jack asked.

Veen walked away without answering.

The new body was simply cloned from the old, since nobody had heard Jemima mentioning modifications. The embryo grew in a container made of cornea, an old tradition from the days when scientists had thought it necessary to have visual control over the child's development.

Jack and Liya went to Jemima's house and stood hand in hand by the growing fetus. Somehow, the tiny and hardly human-like lump of flesh touched Jack more deeply than the memorial.

"Do you want children?" Liya asked as they left.

Jack automatically shook his head. He immediately realized that his swift reaction might have made her sad.

"No," he said, "no, I don't really think so. You?"

She smiled merrily. "Not at all. You know how my childhood was. I just wanted to check. Men can become so emotional when they see a growing embryo."

"Not me. I'm cold and callous."

Later, he thought about it and realized that he actually didn't want children. Not now, anyway. He was fine with Liya, alone together in her house.

Not now. Maybe in his next body.

She joked about his old suggestion of Earth genes.

"You still want to grow coconut palms and plantains? Maybe re-dye the atmosphere?"

"I was wrong," he said. "You just twist that knife."

"Was I out of line?" She suddenly seemed worried.

"Not at all. That was just an idea. Everything's working out much better now.

"Yes," she said, looking out over the brown late summer. "Much better."

That night they watched a romantic holo. Jack first suggested that they'd see it virtually, but Liya wanted to share the experience with him.

The story was traditional. Girl met boy and they fell in love; they broke up; the boy died and had requested an entirely different body; they lost contact, moved further and further away from each other during several bodies as empires grew and collapsed. And finally, they met and joined up again.

Liya was delighted.

"Did you like it?" she said. "I loved it."

Jack didn't love it at all. A run-of-the-mill romance.

"It was okay," he said.

"Oh, I liked those discussions about religion and the multiverse. You know, that thing about a certain percentage of all your versions going to heaven, the rest to hell."

"They could have taken it further," Jack said. "You might imagine that a certain percentage of me, of just *this* edition, goes to heaven. And so on. If you really want to believe that silliness.

"I'd actually like to." She seemed sad for a moment. Then brightened. "But you know what I liked best?"

"No."

"That he was so like you!"

"Who?"

"He. Gabriel. The guy."

"Like me? Him?"

"Yeah! With those kind eyes and the sensitive mouth."

"I have kind eyes?" he said.

"Yes!"

"What, kind?"

"Oh shut up. But he reminded me of you, anyway."

Jack was irritated without really knowing why. "Well, I didn't like that. You can't fall for somebody's looks."

"Of course you can?"

"So you might be with that actor if he was here?"

Her glance was uncertain. "What's the matter? Don't be angry."

Jack breathed deeply and tried to slow his pulse. Biofeedback, stuff he'd worked with since kindergarten.

But this body was very young. It didn't always obey him.

"I'm not angry," he said, just a tad too slow. "I just think that's silly. It's you I love, not your gorgeous looks. Do you think I'm so superficial?"

"But please. Did I say that? I just said that –"

Liya was sad. God, he thought, she really is beautiful.

This made him even angrier: that he himself cared so much for her looks.

They managed to put out the quarrel before it turned into wildfire. They made love, with something that felt like exhaustion, and slept in each other's arms.

That night, Jack dreamed of the holo. The dream placed himself in the male protagonist's, Gabriel's, role; like everybody else, he modified his body for each change; but in his dream the female protagonist, Joanna, had also changed and was unrecognizable. And still they knew each other, a notion that was different from all the holos and virtuals Jack had seen in this genre: in spite of their new bodies, Gabriel and Joanna immediately recognized each other.

The dream was of the kind that lingers, far into the next day. This disturbed Jack. He didn't know why.

While he worked that day, he thought about his background. His dreams were becoming more and more frequent, and somehow it felt as if they had something to do with his memory. He must have thrown a lot of memories away when he left Earth.

Or, he realized, maybe he had saved the memories. On Earth.

The thought wouldn't leave him alone.

There were things he didn't know about himself. They weren't here. But they could be on Earth.

In Finland and in Hawaii, he thought. A cavern in a mountain. Enormous halls, excavated in the cliff, with high shelves full of brain tissue. Among all my memories there might be a truth about myself.

He saw a biological truck roll up to one of the shelves and take down a few containers.

He himself stood at the door. Nervously waiting. The truth was to be relieved.

There was no point to such thoughts. He was fine here. He had Liya and his friends. Sara and Peter at last seemed to have found their peace and almost never fought nowadays. Maybe everybody was settling down in their young bodies.

He worked hard. The first days after the dream, he noticed how he could get stuck in it. The strange thought of recognizing someone in a new body. Longing for something that he couldn't identify. The thought that he was missing some important memory. And the even sillier thought that he had purposefully left those memories on Earth. And so on.

Thus he hid in his work, worked until he was so tired that he couldn't think, and when he and Liya walked home he carefully avoided saying something that might make her sad or reveal his real feelings.

Of course, she saw through him.

"What's the matter?" she asked when they walked home, four days later.

"What?"

"You're so quiet. You work much harder than before, harder than everybody else, as if your life were at stake. What's the great hurry?"

"Nothing. But I, I like to use my body."

She put her arm under his. "I know. And I like it when you use it. But I would like you to use it with me instead of in the mines."

"I'm sorry," he said, "I've just been so tired."

"Yes. That's the problem."

Later that evening:

"You sure you're not up to it?"

"I'm sorry." He felt like he'd said that a hundred times during the evening. "I'll take it easy tomorrow. And tomorrow night. Then."

"I hope so." She kissed him quickly – kissed his forehead, not his mouth – and lay down.

With her back to him. Which immediately felt like she was distancing herself and therefore made him want her. He tentatively caressed her naked shoulder.

"Mmm," she said, and that made him happy. And the joy made his body even more ready.

Later, she said:

"I have to tell you something."

"What?" Although he seemed to be missing some memories, his two hundred years had taught him something about women. Her words, and her tone, were ominous. In all their innocence.

She didn't speak. He became even more nervous.

"Liya."

A deep breath. And then the words came, just a whisper:

"I lied to you."

After a while of questions and some tears, he knew.

She did want to have children. In spite of what she had said.

Centuries had passed and her nineteen-year-old body longed.

"I'm not ready," Jack said.

Which caused more tears.

"Yes," he said at breakfast, "I promise to think about it. It was just so, so sudden last night."

"Do you care for me?"

The ugly duckling, he thought. Strange that that tale still lived, after hundreds of years. It had some kind of power. Just like Liya's own self-doubts. As a child, she hadn't felt loved.

That stayed with her.

Over and over again, he assured her that he loved her and that he really would think about having children. He didn't even know if he was lying.

Coming back from the latrines, he met Veen.

"I've got two now," Veen said.

"Two what?" Jack was miles away.

"Travelers. Going home. Are you interested? If you are, we only need one more."

Jack said, "Let me think about it."

§

His dreams grew. At night, he seemed to drown in them, as if the dreams were endless stormy seas and he a castaway, thrown every which way by wild waves. Now and then the dreams became nightmares and he was speared by jagged cliffs, no doubt inspired by the mountain range where he worked every day. At other times, the storm subsided, and Jack floated alone under a comfortably warm sun; everything was still and he was calm and happy.

At those times, Liya appeared in his dreams. She was suspended above him, her enormous eyes shaped by peculiar cloud formations. At last, he had found peace.

The sea was blue, not reddish brown.

The days were worse. When he awoke and realized that Liya was next to him he felt an immediate tenderness, a longing: the thing he had wanted in his dream was here, in reality, right by his side. But the feeling always dissipated when Liya stirred and looked at him.

He knew the question was coming.

Six days later, it came. Of course, Jack was totally unprepared.

"So have you thought about it?"

"About what?" he said, very aware about what she meant.

She took a deep breath. "If you want children."

They sat at the kitchen table with leftovers between them. Dreams still churned in Jack's head. Liya's blue eyes mirrored the sea within him.

"It's hard ..." He couldn't find anything better to say; even before he opened his mouth, he knew how wrong the words were.

Liya turned away.

He tried that evening.

"Can you give me a little time?" he said. "It's all so new. I never thought about kids before. Not on Earth and not here."

"You're a man."

"Far as I know." He tried to smile but she didn't smile back; she wouldn't even look at him.

"It's much more biological for women. Reproduction, I mean. It's built into us."

"That might be modified."

"I know. But I chose not to." She suddenly looked him straight in the eye. "Have you modified yourself? To not want kids?"

He shook his head. "I never thought about it. Not in any of my bodies. As I said."

The matter came up again.

"It's my fault?" she said. "Right? It's my fault. I'm so unsure of myself that I nag you to pieces."

"Well, in that case," he tried, "that's what you're doing right now. When you ask if it's your fault."

"I know. But I want you to answer."

"It's not your fault."

That night, he slept in his own empty house.

In the morning, Jack went to Liya's house and tactfully knocked on her door. Nothing moved inside. He stood there for a couple of minutes and then knocked again. Nothing. He left.

Outside his own house he saw Veen. Veen was on his way toward the mines but immediately turned when he saw that Jack was alone.

"Jack," he said from ten feet away. Still in a low voice. "Jack, I have one more. The guy from Korea. If you're in, we can go as soon as the ships are ready."

"I'll think about it."

But he already knew his mind was made up.

When he told her, Liya silently cried.

"You can come too," Jack tried.

"You don't want me to."

"Of course I do."

She sniffled, red-eyed. "Don't lie to me. At least give me that."

He thought. Tried to soften the blow. "I don't know what it is. It's something inside me. You have your years as an ugly duckling. I have something else, something that I can't really understand. I don't know which is worse."

"You don't care for me."

"I love you a lot." He took her hand and looked in her eyes: he was sure that he wasn't lying, this last time. "I love you. Very much. But I have to solve this problem within myself. Do you understand?"

She said nothing, just sobbed silently again.

"I may come back," he tried, "in a couple of hundred years. When I've solved this. And you've solved your problems. And all will end well."

"This isn't a holo. Idiot."

He held his hands up. Gave in.

They lived apart during the few months it took to modify their houses back to ships again. The process could have been faster, but the colony wasn't overwhelmed with the concept of investing time and work in people that were leaving.

Jack slept alone and worked alone. He lived in his dreams.

He met the other travelers once or twice. But they would travel in stasis and had no need to be friendly, Veen, the Korean and two Siberian brothers. Everybody nodded politely but nobody started unnecessary conversations.

Jack missed Liya. Still, he couldn't make himself visit her. That would have been cruel to both of them.

At last, the day of departure came.

The houses had slowly parceled off unnecessary material, separated from their neighbors, been dragged together and then united as a ship. Jack tried to joke with one of the technicians about the risks for going back to Earth unmodified, as a terribly gaunt miniature human; the technician gave him a blank look and Jack quit joking.

Downloading his memories from Shylock through the biological interface took some time. Jack lay immovable, waiting.

The next time he stood up he would literally be a new human being. And he would be home on Earth.

A soft bleating signaled that memory transfer was almost ready. The technician activated the penultimate drip.

Jack said good-bye to his body. He knew that he would remember even these last minutes. All the way until sleepiness overcame him and the sleeping drug was replaced by poison.

This had been a good body, he thought sleepily. Pity that his soul hadn't worked out equally well.

Right now, this body was actually dying. But there was no anxiety, no worry or fear. Just drowsiness and whirling dreams.

Jack saw Liya's face in front of him. He wished her luck.

He quietly died.

6

Once again, he was everything. Without boundaries between his self and the surrounding world. He was everything and everywhere.

Slowly waking. An eternal moment.

He lay there, sunken in amniotic fluid, peacefully rocking while fragments of what would later make up his self floated in another way, in his conscience, colliding and joining. Fell apart, floated on, melted together again.

The state just after waking. When consciousness and self reform after having been lost for one night or seventy-three years.

He remembered who he was. That he'd been on the planet Shylock. That he'd given up his little body there and that the new body which he was slowly making contact with, while he got to know his hands and feet again, as sensory tendrils that sent impulses back to his mind when he ordered them to bend fingers and toes – that the new body was different.

Different but familiar.

This was a body like the ones he'd had on Earth before. Larger and heavier. Not as wispy as the one he'd lived in on Shylock. He imagined that he could feel the weight, still floating in liquid.

He remembered something else.

Liya's eyes.

Liya herself.

He let himself float away again.

The next time, more came back. No, he realized, he hadn't chosen to erase Liya, painful though it all had been. He wondered why. The memories were wistful. Liya had trusted him and he had let her down.

But he had let her down, he immediately reminded himself, because he had to. He hadn't been feeling well on the desolate planet.

He contemplated, sleepily. If it had been legal, he could have left his little thin body alive on Shylock. It could have lived there with Liya while this edition built a new future on Earth.

But that was illegal. It might cause quite strange problems: what would have happened if Jack had left a copy of himself on Shylock, a copy who had lived with Liya, and if the Jack that had gone back to Earth then had changed his mind and gone back to the colony planet? Who would be who? Which one should Liya live with? How to solve all other problems with laws and customs? The simplest solution was to outlaw the possibility.

Their ship landed in Europe, in the old city of Orléans, and took some tests. Everything worked as it should. Jack had chosen to be twenty-four years old, not as hormonally explosive as on Shylock but still young and strong. The other colonists stayed at nineteen.

After testing, they were asked questions about Shylock. The world was very interested, they were told: when colonists returned home they always had to tell their story in as much detail as possible, and of course share all holos – except very private ones – that they'd recorded.

Earth did nothing for colonists on other planets. If the colonies expired they expired. But people who returned home could be interesting news.

Jack answered questions. He listened to stories of other colonies, those that had expired and those that were still alive, and soon understood that the purpose wasn't to inform him – it was to check his reactions.

Jack listened and answered politely. But within him, impatience grew. He wanted to know.

A day later he flew north in a biological plane, not unlike the ship where his genes and memories had traveled for one hundred and forty-six years.

He'd been gone for one hundred and forty-seven years and only lived one of these on Shylock.

The one hundred and forty-seven years could be seen on his home planet. He flew over old Oresund and noticed that the sea had receded: when Jack left for Shylock, most of the lands around the Sound had still been under water.

Jack imagined the sunken cities, old stone buildings, cathedrals and mansions, covered by billowing sea-grass while green sunlight filtered down from the surface in slanted streaks and scared shoals of swift fish.

He saw more change as he came further north. Less wasteland, more forests and farmland. From the plane, it seemed as if every little strip of land was utilized.

But then, even further north, the farms slowly were replaced by tundra.

Jack was impatient. He took out a leaflet that he'd been given at the testing clinic in Orléans and read about the Earth's population doubling during the last century. Authorities expressed hope that colonization should grow before resources went scarce again. The leaflet was boring and he let it fall to the floor.

He'd soon know. And his impatience grew by the minute.

Jack was headed for a town in old Finland, not too far from the Torne River, once marking the border between Finland in the east and Sweden in the west. The town was called Rovaniemi and held one copy of Jack's memories.

Rovaniemi had grown. When Jack had left the place after depositing his memories, it had consisted of ruins from the 21st century and a small core of living buildings. Now all the ruins had disappeared. The organic buildings had kept growing, like weeds, he thought, and covered everything.

More and more, he realized how much his home planet had changed. Still, many things were the same. Cities abandoned during the upheavals were growing again. With the exception of people like Veen, humans sought other humans. People wanted to live close to people, to see their humanity mirrored in others. Maybe this was a necessary feedback process. Maybe humans had to see themselves mirrored in others to be human, to become human.

As Jack was shown into the well-protected subterranean room where his memories waited, he thought about the almost one hundred and fifty years that had passed. Before the multis came, at least four or five generations of humans would have lived and died during the time he had been gone. Now all those generations, and many older ones, lived simultaneously.

A woman let him into the vault. Her body was greatly modified. She had ears and eyes like a cat: vertical pupils and upright ears that peeped out through her hair. Her whiskers fascinated him.

"It's common now," she said in her singsong dialect. "I can see you're staring. It's a trend. You'll see it many times."

Even before the white door silently closed behind him, Jack knew that something was wrong. To store memories from two hundred years, he could not have needed more than four or possibly five brains.

There were almost twenty brains in the vault.

Calling them "brains" was technically not correct. They weren't complete. But nobody but experts could tell the difference.

Jack counted them. Eighteen brains, each in its jar, quietly floating in nutritional fluid.

Once again, he wondered if the brains dreamed.

"I can help you," the cat woman said amiably. "If you don't remember how –"

"I'm all right," he interrupted. "Please leave." He hadn't meant it to sound that harsh. The woman nodded and left without saying anything more.

He thought about calling her back but discarded the notion. He couldn't wait any longer.

The brains were far too many. And something else was wrong.

The jars where the brains floated had no labels.

You didn't really label your brains like antique photo albums:

"Holiday in South east Asia, spring 2643."

"Liya and me by the sea on Shylock."

He wondered why Liya appeared in his thoughts again. Guilty conscience, he thought, no doubt a guilty conscience.

Very few people wrote such labels. But memories at least used to be labeled with years.

He thought about calling for the cat-faced woman. Maybe the labeling system had simply changed. Whatever.

Then he shrugged.

You linked up to the memory banks with cables of nerve fiber. When Jack connected the fiber behind his left ear, he felt the normal moment of giddiness.

Then it got worse.

He might have been sixteen years old. It was hard to know for sure, but his body looked that way.

He could see something else, too.

There was a lot less biological material in this world. Even that was wrong. The childhood he remembered hadn't been like that.

Here, houses were built of wood and stone. Machines of metal roared on enormous roads of melted and cast stone. Other machines roared even louder, high in the air.

People screamed and cried. Smoke rose from buildings close by and far away. People in green uniforms shouted and pointed. Others were running away or trying to hide.

In Jack's memories on Shylock, there had been no wars.

He recognized the soldiers' uniforms from holos and virtuals and realized that he was in the middle of the upheavals.

Then his mother died, right in front of him.

It was pure chance that he even saw it. He happened to look her way at the very moment the shrapnel split her head. She fell straight down – even in that situation, Jack thought of her not falling slowly like dying people in holos and virtuals. His mother fell immediately, straight down, like a stone.

Jack yanked out the nerve fiber with no preparation, without even thinking. He tottered but managed to regain his balance again.

His breathing was ragged.

His mother. During the upheavals. Seven hundred years ago.

He had thought he'd been born centuries later. That was wrong. He knew that was wrong because he could relive these memories without hurting his brain: they were his own, he knew this and he felt it.

After just a few seconds, the impact of the stored memory began to fade. He tried to hold on to his mother's face but it trickled away, sliding off between the synapses in his head.

She had died. And five hundred fifty years of memory, seven hundred years minus his trip to Shylock, waited in the jars before him.

Could this be what had whispered to him on Shylock? No, he immediately thought; no, never. This memory was ghastly. He was surprised he had saved it at all.

There must be something else in the jars. Something he really longed for, enough to make it call for him across thirty-two light-years.

He wondered why the labels were gone. What was the advantage in that?

Maybe there were, he thought, some new rules.

"No," the cat-eyed woman said, "it was your own wish." The woman was a little more reserved now, still polite, but in a guarded way. "All labels would be removed and no references at all could be kept."

Jack nodded.

"Do you have anything left?" he said. "In writing? Some documents?"

She considered and then looked in an enormous filing cabinet. He waited. After a couple minutes, she gave him an old document.

Jack read.

She was right.

"There must have been something you wanted to forget," she said. Jack nodded impatiently.

He had suspected that already on Shylock. He also had an idea about *what* he had forgotten. But he wanted to know for sure.

The answer was in the vault.

One of the things that had changed was that he was immensely rich. He found this out when the woman helped him to check his accounts.

He did remember a great fortune even when he had left. Now, he learned that it was two hundred times larger.

"Interest?" the whiskered woman suggested.

He quickly calculated and then shook his head. Interest wasn't sufficient.

"I must have hidden my funds from myself," he said.

The woman gave him a questioning look.

He flew home the next morning. Carrying eighteen brains in the luggage compartment.

The plane was chartered. That cost quite a lot. But money, he noted, was the least of his troubles.

Home was a place that had been famous even before the upheavals: the biggest rapids in this part of the world left untouched by water power plants.

This Jack had known already before he connected the nerve fiber and remembered himself as a sixteen-year-old. His estate had been a nice joke and he had carried that memory to Shylock.

He had known that he owned all the land between Storforsen, as the place still was called, and the ancient town of Älvsbyn. What he hadn't known was that he had owned this land for seven hundred years.

When he left for Shylock, this land had been more or less worthless. The sea had licked its way almost up to the forgotten town and the only thing that remained after the forest had been cleared was wastelands. Wastelands and tundra.

But nature could change quite a lot in one hundred and fifty years.

Jack sat alone in the passenger compartment and looked down on his land. The first things he passed were forests and farms, assets needed to make cultivated DNA grow. Some employee must have taken care of all this for him, slowly making his fortune grow in step with his forests.

Further west, the forest ended. The ground turned to gray tundra.

One of the things he didn't remember was his home. When he saw the building, he forgot everything about economy. He stared.

It turned out the place was still famous. Not just because of the great rapids, still foaming between the banks of the river, but also because of the unlikely building that was Jack's home.

"Very famous," the cabin hostess said. She also had cat-like features, making her smile strange. "A copy of Hatshepsut's death temple."

Jack's face must have mirrored the emptiness in his brain.

"Egypt?" the hostess said, her smile wavering a little. "Deir-el Bahri, outside old Luxor?"

"I'm sorry, but ..."

"Oh, you don't have to excuse yourself," the hostess said quickly. "I'll get you some leaflets. Enjoy the view."

At first, he had thought it was snow. The season was early spring and when he left this world, it hadn't been unusual for snow to remain at this time.

But it wasn't snow.

To the north of the great rapids, on his right side as they closed in from the east, was an immense white surface. Each flat surface was a kind of courtyard, the largest at the bottom, the smallest on the top.

The levels were divided by high walls, where portals stood in line. Gigantic ramps led from the lowest level up to the highest.

Everything rose from the gray-brown tundra. Behind the building, the ground ascended in soft slopes to the right of the swirling rapids. The scenery was stunning.

"And it's all yours," the cabin hostess said, smiling.

He didn't know what to say.

Next to the lowest and largest flat surface was a little airfield. The plane didn't need much time to take to the air again. Jack stood there, first looking at the ascending plane and then staring at the building.

The hostess had told him all this was alive. Made from his own biological material.

He walked carefully on the sun-heated enamel. A man with a supple but somehow different body came to meet him, quickly walking down the wide ramp.

The man called something. Jack couldn't make out the words. He was too fascinated with what he saw. The young man had the face of a lynx, complete with tufts of hair on his upright ears; he had a human's hands but lynx' paws instead of feet.

"I thought you'd never come home again," said the modified man who said he was Jack's own son. "But then I had a message from Rovaniemi."

"Well, I didn't think I meant to." Jack didn't know how much to tell him.

"It didn't seem like it. You lived with a woman between AD 2551 and 2556. Her name was Maya." The young man seemed quite formal for a son. "You had two sons with her. I'm the older. My brother is called Ben –"

"Excuse me. What did you say your name was?"

"You don't have to excuse yourself. I'm Joss." The smile seemed as young as the face, even if Joss had to be almost two hundred years old. But then, this wasn't his first body. He had chosen his lynx appearance himself.

Jack nodded politely.

"So Ben and I have shared responsibility for your lands and this place since, in periods of ten or twenty years."

"Doesn't it get lonely?" Jack said when his son ran out of breath.

"Here?" Joss said enthusiastically. "If you only knew –" His lynx face suddenly seemed to blush. When he went on, he sounded a tad defensive. "Well, you never said we had to live like hermits. And this place is known all over the world."

"Guests? Parties?"

"Guests. And parties."

Jack studied his son. Yes, by now he could recognize some of his own features. In spite of the modifications.

Idly, he wondered who Ben's mother had been. The memories of her were somewhere in the big carts unloaded from the plane. But he didn't feel very curious.

He must have had his sons as a kind of investment. Like building a new house or acquiring new biological machines.

He felt no fatherly love. What he had said to Liya was true, he realized. He wasn't that interested in reproduction.

His son smiled. "I guess modifications were less common when you left."

It dawned upon Jack that he was staring. "Hm," he said vaguely. "Excuse me if I'm ..."

"No worry."

Jack wanted to change the subject.

"But you, you and you brother ... you have had salaries."

The lynx smiled. "Princely ones, you might say."

"Princely?"

"Unknown word? Fair-sized. Big. Salaries for princes?"

"I see." Jack thought. "I'd like to be alone here," he said. "For a time. A few weeks, maybe longer, I don't know. You can keep your salaries, but you and Beck –"

"Ben."

"Ben. You still are my sons." He tried to smile but didn't really succeed. "I want to be alone here. Alone with my memories."

They turned to look at the big carts, waiting to be rolled into the temple.

His son left early next morning; Jack didn't know how. Joss had seemed a little interested, maybe dutifully, in talking and spending time together the night before, but Jack had impatiently asked to be left alone.

He didn't know this young man. He had no memory of his mother.

The genes were his but there was no personal connection.

Maybe they would build one. But right now, Jack was uninterested. He had other plans.

He thought of the people he'd met since coming home and thought: I might not be a very nice person.

Joss had helped him to place the jars in a storage room that was fitted-up and ready.

"Can I ask you something?" the young man had said.

"Yes?"

"Why did you store your memories in Rovaniemi? Why not here?"

Jack thought for a moment. Then he shrugged.

"It seems like I was trying to hide my own past. When I was on Shylock, my memory was that I was two hundred years old."

"Two hundred! That's far too –"

"I know," Jack said. "I think I was born before the upheavals."

"My mother tells me that."

Jack nodded. "And I wanted to hide all that from myself."

"But no longer."

"No," Jack said. "No longer."

Jack had slept on the top floor. There were more than thirty bedrooms in what he was increasingly thinking about as his palace.

He walked two floors down. The morning sun shone in the east and enamel glittered blindingly in the light.

Eighteen silent brains waited for him.

There were two ways of accessing memories, not unlike holos and virtuals. You could either watch your visual and aural memories being replayed or live through them.

Like most people, Jack was quite careful about living through memories. Memories were stored in living brains; even before the upheavals it had been known that memories changed; even today, memories would change inside your head, so that you couldn't always be sure that a memory was a memory – or if it was just a memory of a memory.

And in that case, how much of it was still real.

By choosing to just replay the memories, only see and hear, with a simple one-way connection between memory bank and brain, you could keep them unchanged. With a two-way connection, that made it possible to relive events with thoughts and feelings, your own new reactions to your old reactions could change the stored experience. In a desired way, or an undesired – but anyway, away from what once had been real.

Jack chose one-way replay. He had another reason, too.

The memory of his mother still tormented him. Unmoving and dead on the ground, blood still pulsing. The picture had affected him in a bad way, even if it was only a replay. If he'd chosen to live through that memory, he was afraid he might have damaged his psyche.

And somewhere among these eighteen gray-pale clumps was something that he must have wanted to hide, to run away from, even more than he wanted to escape the memory of his mother's death.

He began his search.

He had been born in 2032. About ten or fifteen years before the upheavals, depending on which writing of history you preferred.

He had lived through the upheavals.

His mother had died. Her name had been Helena, not Alina, as he'd called her in the memories he'd brought to Shylock. She had been killed at the age of forty-two.

His father had survived the wars but not the famine afterwards. Magnus, born in 1992.

The twentieth century. Ancient ages.

He was fascinated.

What he'd replayed became memories in his present brain, just like he remembered holos he'd seen. He gradually rebuilt his life.

Since memory worked like a hologram he went into a kaleidoscope every time he connected the fiber to a new memory bank. Faces, names, places and events all whirled, at first without any context; then he chose a face or an event and could see memories get organized.

Still, it wasn't easy to understand everything.

He worked for days. Over and over again, he returned to brains that he'd already searched, connecting events that at first had seemed incomprehensible with new data, understanding a little more.

He wished that he hadn't needed this many brains. But they were a safety measure. Long ago, it had been understood that the one cause for senility was simply overloading the brain. The storage capacity was filled and started to leak. Memories muddled together and were erased.

And the latest memories went first.

His seven hundred years might have been squeezed into seven or even four brains. But this might have made his stored memories senile, made them degenerate into impossible nonsense from his childhood.

He found more. How he'd made it through the upheavals. How he had gotten rich and how he'd managed his fortune.

It was in the morning of the fourth day he saw her. And sorrow returned.

7

Of course, it was a woman. He had suspected that even on Shylock.

He noticed that it still hurt. Not just the so to speak academic or theoretical pain you could experience when you saw news about catastrophes, death and horror. This struck harder.

Straight to the heart.

It was there. He knew he could find it. But he also knew that he'd been fleeing from this memory for centuries. He needed strength.

He walked on blinding enamel. The reflected sun was high in the south. Summer solstice was close.

I need strength, he thought. I can wait. I can start by going through my other memories.

What happened before.

From now on, he took his time. His random and almost feverish samples had given him a kind of general picture of his real life.

And one special picture, a picture of a young woman with large and widely spaced eyes. A face that refused to leave him alone.

Of course, she looked quite like Liya.

But the picture of the girl would have to wait. He wanted to prepare, to get ready; or maybe he just wanted to spin out time, postpone his delight as long as possible.

He replayed his life.

The upheavals had started a little before the year 2050. Jack had been fourteen when they reached northern Sweden.

"This is going to hell," his father had said.

Jack's father had been a musician and still lived off royalties from his short but radiant career. He had been so intensely waiting for civilization to break down that he almost welcomed it happening.

It was called upheavals but it had been more like the end of the world. At least for about nine of the Earth's ten billion people who were killed, or died from famine or epidemics.

Many factors caused the upheavals, but the two most important were polar caps finally melting and different kinds of oil finally running out. When sea levels rose many feet, islands and coastal areas became uninhabitable. At the same time, the last wars for oil took place. Dog ate dog: small countries entered their even smaller neighbors to grab the last drops of oil but were themselves quickly invaded by the United States or China, the time's greatest powers. Protesters were killed by the thousands both outside government buildings and at the enclaves which the world's richest had created for themselves – at some places, the protesters kept thronging like the zombies that had been so popular at the time, climbing on each other's dying bodies, biting and clawing, sometimes overcoming the armed guards and reaching the cowering billionaires' unsafe havens, raging and killing.

Many waited for the nuclear war. That never happened – at least not in the full-scale version that people had feared for a hundred years. It was true that a few warheads detonated when the US obliterated some small oil-producing states, in some kind of vague hope to be able to exploit the last resources in the ground when the radiation had subsided. But radiation didn't have the time to subside before both the US and China had dissolved into many small feudal states, which squandered even more oil and technology, and millions of human lives.

A few last warheads exploded but the final war never happened. At last, there were too few people left to fight it.

Jack watched the memory of his mother's death again, just to understand.

It had happened several centuries ago, but the memory was fresh and clear and still hurt.

The war had finally reached their little town in the north. The US had decided to invade the Norwegians to take their oil. Whatever good that may have done them; maybe a couple more years of squandering.

For some reason, the USA also chose to attack from land, and for this they needed bases in Sweden. The Vidsel air base just north of Jack's town could have been the reason why this town was attacked. And for some reason, the Swedish government tried to fight back – "a mouse braving a lion," as some opposition politician had said before being arrested.

What was the point? Jack wondered as he watched his memories. This time he was more attentive to details, recognized American fighter planes and tanks, uniforms.

But at last, he couldn't bear watching his mother's death again. He disconnected just seconds before.

Afterwards he breathed deeply, bending over with his head almost between his legs, out on the enormous white surface, before the copy of the Egyptian queen's temple.

On Shylock, he had had vague memories of his mother. Those pictures were wrong.

Now he knew that she was as dead as the Egyptian queen.

He wondered what had happened to his father. The only memory he could find was some unknown person saying that Magnus had died in the famine.

Maybe this is better, Jack thought, than knowing exactly how he died.

The amount of death and destruction in the mid-21st century was appalling. The world was a pit of stinking corpses and burned-out buildings. Jack wondered how he himself had survived.

One day, maybe his seventh or eighth in the temple, a multi appeared. The creature glittered transparently in the searing sunshine.

"Tell me how I survived," Jack said. But the multi didn't have an answer. At least, it didn't send any pictures.

The multi floated behind him into the temple. Into the room Jack had begun calling the grave chamber. Where his embalmed memories rested.

In his memories he saw his young self – his eyes had seen everything except his own face, apart from the times when he'd happened to look in mirrors – managing to get along while he, surprisingly, considering the lack of food, grew bigger and stronger. He smiled at himself, being nineteen for the first time: he had already forgotten how his body on Shylock, thin as a thread, had looked and felt, and only remembered the storming hormones that he could see so clearly in this boy's behavior.

His memories showed him a new world, slowly appearing.

At first, the new world was poor and strenuous. He had been in his early twenties when the violence and epidemics faded. The Internet, the electronic communications net that had helped to keep the world together like a pressure bandage up to 2048, was long dead and abandoned. There were small feudal princes here and there with private electrical generators, first run by petroleum, then by wood fires; but the gadgets using electricity became more and more scarce, ran out, broke, stopped working.

The new world became medieval.

Without communication by motor vehicles, the Internet or phones, it was impossible to keep together countries of Sweden or Finland's size, let alone the US or China. Instead, small feudal realms appeared. Their masters or mistresses ruled land areas of maybe fifty square miles and had armies of maybe hundreds or a few thousands of men. During the first years, treachery was common: two feudal lords attacked a third, or an army joined their neighbor's realm. But within a decade or so, a kind of fragile equilibrium had been reached.

Young Jack became a slave for a small feudal lord. The man was called Roger and wasn't any more cruel than anybody else. Jack's memories showed a number of hangings and whippings and he quickly fast-forwarded past these.

Then it happened: Jack did something unforgivable, something forbidden; he didn't seem to understand quite what his crime was, but he knew what the whipping meant. As well as the noose ceremonially laid around his neck.

He was thrown into a cold and damp cell, hands and feet tied, the noose still tight around his throat, to suffer one last night.

The older Jack could have stopped replaying his memories there. He didn't. He knew he wouldn't die now: he knew this, since the memories existed.

He couldn't help watching while his seven centuries younger self writhed and trembled from cold, eyes just inches from the ice-cold floor.

His vision blurred and the Jack replaying the memories knew he was crying.

Then, something appeared in the cell. Something undefined, shimmering, something that may have been solid in the middle but whose blurred edges may or may not have existed in our universe.

A multi.

The younger Jack didn't notice it at first, although it was right in his field of vision. He was still trying to curb his shaking.

The Jack watching the memory suddenly straightened.

He had always – that was, since he'd traveled to Shylock – believed, and heard others say, that multis didn't appear until the beginning of the 22nd century.

This was more than fifty years earlier.

The multi did something shimmering and the heavy door opened. Then it slid over to Jack and did something else.

Jack was free.

The present Jack wondered what his younger self could have thought. Maybe he had believed that the multi was a ghost. Some kind of spirit. Or maybe that it was some kind of war robot, preserved and activated right here.

A blurry picture appeared before the prisoner's eyes. It showed Jack sneaking out of the cell to where, in the corridor, the two guards were posted.

The guards were fast asleep and the young Jack silently slipped past them.

Outside, a quickly nailed-together gallows waited. Jack only saw it out of the corner of his eye. His pace quickened and he went into the woods.

He had been walking through the woods for a week. From time to time, he saw people and avoided them. He found roots and berries to eat. Once he saw a dead squirrel, but the day-old carcass made his stomach turn.

At last, he came to another mansion. That was where he met her. The girl called Rachel.

The older Jack quickly scanned his memories. He had worked at the farm an entire winter. With time, he'd won the feudal lord's confidence and became a foreman. His thin arms and legs had slowly filled out.

Every now and then, he saw a glimpse of the girl.

She was unattainable. Class boundaries were more pronounced in the new world than in the old. There were a few nobles, or whatever you wanted to call them, with families, living in the great mansion; somewhere between forty and fifty people. They had their trusted friends and subjects. At the bottom of the scale, below the paid soldiers, were the workers, including foremen like Jack.

Rachel was the lord's daughter. She was also the most beautiful girl Jack had ever seen. At first, he didn't seem to search her out – he only happened to look at her, sometimes, at a distance. Months would go by before he even exchanged a few words with her.

This happened in summer, right after Jack had become a fore-man. He didn't have to live in a drafty barracks any more. Instead he shared a warmer room with Tom, the other foreman. Tom was older than Jack and also bigger and stronger. Luckily, they got along fine.

One morning, Jack was on his way out to the arid fields when Rachel hurried up to him. She wore a white summer dress, reaching halfway to her knees, which looked homemade. Even seven hund-red years later, she was absolutely and totally stunning.

"You're Jack, right?"

"Yeah." He avoided meeting her gaze – probably, he was too awed.

"Where's Tom?"

"I don't know. In the fields?"

"He was supposed to drive me to the lake."

The lord, Matti, had an old car, run by wood-gas and still wor-king. Jack didn't know what to say.

"Can you drive me?" Rachel said impatiently.

"I can't drive," Jack mumbled.

"What did you say? Look at me when you speak to me." She was younger than Jack, just under twenty, but already used to giving orders.

"I can't drive." Jack met her gaze. She nodded curtly and stomped away, obviously irritated.

Her eyes were large and dark and widely spaced. The mouth also was big, with full lips that even today made the older Jack weak in his knees. When she hurried away, his younger self dared to look at her. Hundreds of years later, replaying the memory as a holo, he couldn't remember what he'd thought. But the way his eyes roamed as she went told him what the young man's hormones were doing.

After that, he must have begun dreaming of her.

The older Jack stopped the playback.

Those eyes still unsettled him.

Somehow he'd remembered them, although he'd stowed these

memories away. He had been dreaming about Rachel's eyes. And he'd been attracted to Liya because she reminded him of this girl.

Jack chose another memory bank.

He marked up every brain that he checked. "Childhood" marked two jars; "Upheavals" a third. The one he'd just played got a simple "R."

Jack wanted to know more about multis. After two trials with brains that were a lot younger, he found the right one.

The other two brains were also full of Rachel. Memories of Rachel, and long sequences with his younger self staring into walls or up at the sky. It wasn't hard to guess what he was dreaming about.

Jack decided to avoid them. For a while.

He had to find another brain – he labeled it "Multis" – before the picture cleared.

It was true that multis had become known on Earth in the early 2100's. But before that, they had had contact with a few chosen people. Jack had been one of these.

He could very well have been the first.

The second time he met a multi was when he'd left Matti's mansion, no doubt carrying Rachel with him like an open and bleeding wound. He'd wandered south, as close to the new coast as he could, during a mild winter. Once in a while, he did day work for peasants or hunters, and he'd also learned how to steal food.

One day he stood on a mountainside, seeing settlements in front of him. He was debating whether he ought to show himself when he reacted and looked to his right.

The multi glittered indistinctly next to him.

"Who are you?" Jack said.

The multi shimmered and Jack saw a picture in front of himself. The picture was obscure and faint and the older Jack couldn't quite recognize it. Then it clicked.

A double helix.

"DNA?" his young self said. Old Jack remembered seeing such pictures in school.

A new picture emerged. It showed himself. Naked, as the pictures of humans sent into space some decades before he had been born. Next to him was a multi.

Something left Jack's body, grew and formed a shape. It was the double helix. It slid over to the creature next to Jack. The multi in the picture had no discernable limbs or other body parts, but the double seemed to know its way and disappeared into the shimmering being.

"For what?" Jack said. "I mean –"

Next to the multi in the picture two other beings appeared, but only half as big. They seemed to be children or descendants. The grown multi in the picture gave Jack's DNA to them.

The smaller ones began playing with the double helix. They threw it back and forth between each other, stretching it, changing its shape.

"A plaything?" Jack said. "DNA as a toy?"

Later, he met others who shared that experience. Nobody had ever hesitated about giving their genetic material to the blurry creatures.

Everyone had been richly compensated.

During a period of several years, while he wandered in a world being born again, Jack met multis from time to time. They took his DNA, most often simply by having him spit at some kind of limb or tentacle that blurred out to him, sometimes by taking a hair or by scraping off some skin.

Being touched by a multi was a strange feeling. Sometimes there would be a burning sensation, but mostly the touch was light as a feather, somehow tickling. It was there and it wasn't, just like visual impressions of the creature.

The multi helped Jack learn who he was.

With time, he started thinking of himself as somebody with a weak ego. He didn't know at all if this term might be correct; he thought he'd coined it himself, just to have a term; he guessed that psychologists before the upheavals might have meant something completely different by the term.

To Jack, the term meant that he lived quite as much in his imagination as in reality. When the younger Jack thought of his life and talked to others – his fantasies while growing up, the fear of being hanged at Roger's farm, his dreams of the unattainable Rachel – his older self could sometimes hear him mentioning how big a part of his life fantasies were and had been.

He had begun thinking that that was the reason why the multis had chosen him. His closeness to his dreams made him a suitable recipient for their gift.

A multi showed him that the gift was a virus. By now, Jack had come to trust the multis. When the multi showed pictures of Jack putting his tongue out, he obeyed; the tip of his tongue burned when the top part of the stooped multi touched him in something that might have been a kiss; Jack uncertainly smacked his lips but felt no taste.

After that, he learned to rebuild people.

Actually, this development was quite natural. Before the upheavals, humans had used tools to extend their bodies, block and tackle and levers to increase their power, field glasses to see at a distance, wheels and motors for faster travel, at last computers and the Internet for communication. During the early 2000's, it had also grown more and more common to rebuild bodies: breasts and lips changed by implants, genitals and faces reshaped.

But this was something else.

The virus that Jack had received from the multis, a race whose children seemed to use human DNA as a plaything, made it possible to rebuild the very cells from scratch. By activating codons in new ways, living organisms could be changed.

Multis appeared with Jack from time to time, showing him what he should do. He had to transport himself to a hypnagogic state, a world of dreams between sleep and waking, and then simply dream what he wanted until it became real.

And it happened.

Jack had never liked his eyes. In mirrors, he stared at them and made faces. They actually were kind of watery and deep-set. His older self could sometimes hear him hinting, never saying straight out, that maybe this one girl might have been drawn to him if his eyes hadn't been so ugly.

Lying half asleep, he imagined new and better eyes, bright blue, curious and frank.

A few months went by without anything happening. He didn't see any change. But one night, at an inn outside a town that had once been called Kramfors, one of the barmaids approached him, plainly letting him know what she wanted. Jack was alone and wanted the same.

Afterwards, the girl said:

"It was your eyes. I just couldn't resist your eyes."

Jack looked into the mirror in the girl's room and met a pair of dizzyingly blue and attractive eyes.

He tried other things. He dreamed himself free of the common colds he had been prone to all his life. The ugly scars from his whipping at Roger's place disappeared within weeks when he started dreaming of soft and smooth skin. He made himself a little straighter, a little taller; he didn't know if his posture was related to genes, but the important thing was that it got better.

He gave himself a more powerful sexual charisma and shared beds with many other girls and women, bargirls and others.

But he was getting older. He was fifty-three when he decided to rejuvenate his body. During that summer, he hid in the woods, let nobody see him while his hair turned black again and his wrinkles faded. Every night he dreamed of himself as a young boy, although taller and with striking eyes. And his dreams came true.

8

The technique spread quickly but not always smoothly. The older Jack stared wide-eyed at a memory of a middle-aged man who had wanted to cure his loss of hair, but who hadn't learned to control his genetic make-up safely: he was found in his bed, totally covered by long coarse hair that had grown everywhere, even in little tufts from nails and eyeballs, and filled all of his inner organs, including trachea and lungs. By this time, Jack already had had a certain reputation; he had been called to the place but it was too late.

The authorities which were slowly growing again at first were critical. In time, however, the ruling classes realized the advantages of controlling diseases and lengthening life-spans, not least for themselves, and the negative voices soon went quiet.

Rumors of strange incidents spread; a man somewhere in the north was said to have shot at a multi with an old rifle; afterwards, an enormous pool of blood was said to remain, but the multi disappeared without a trace.

Many people thought that humanity must try to reach the level of the multis. New meditation centers were started, but no human managed to reach the nirvana of the multiverse.

"Animals also live in the multiverse," Jack heard a woman say one evening, in one of the inns which gradually seemed to become his habitat. "They have no consciousness and see everything that can happen. That's why they never worry. They know everything is happening, and happening simultaneously."

"You mean multis have no conscience?" the man opposite her said. Both their bodies were altered: the woman had luminous owl eyes; the man's body was thick as a tree trunk, covered with biological tattoos that shimmered and changed as if he had been a multi.

"No, didn't you know? They live in an eternal now. As humans did a few thousand years ago, before we got stuck in our consciousness. Maybe we also could move freely in the multiverse at that time."

The man shook his head.

"God is dead," he said in his bass rumble.

"And man has become divine."

This was the first time Jack heard such theories but not the last. More and more people came to believe that consciousness played a part.

Again, people experimented, and again, the experiments gave the most unexpected and sometimes horrific results. But nobody managed to raise humanity either to divinity or to the level of the multis.

Jack disconnected the nerve fiber. He stood. Yawned and stretched.

A multi towered before him. Jack had been sitting under a roof, facing the enormous enamel terrace. The multi blocked the sun. Outside its dark kernel it seemed transparent.

The multi said and did nothing. Jack couldn't say if it was watching him. Nobody could tell if multis had some kind of visual organ – although their use of pictures indicated that they did.

The creature shimmered in place, the sun shining through it, while Jack heated water on his biological hot plate and made coffee. When Jack turned to it again it was gone.

"Cheers," Jack said.

Things changed faster. After about a century, Jack changed bodies for the first time; he had rejuvenated himself a few times but this took time and the process was troublesome. He cultivated a new body and learned to transfer memories and consciousness to it.

He was seventeen again. But with an older man's experience.

This was strange. Even stranger was seeing it happen seven hundred years later. Jack slowly realized how many lives were stored in abandoned brains.

Young Jack wasn't the only experimenter. Within decades, nearly all humans stored memories and changed bodies when their old ones grew tired; or when they wanted to change sexes or enjoy themselves in some other way.

Some of them mixed in genes from animals. The woman with the yellow owl eyes was one of the first Jack saw. A couple of decades later there was a period when many humans adopted traits from animals, like deer-girls or bull-men. Many tried creating different kinds of wings, but flying was hard in Earth's atmosphere and gravity.

At first, it had only been possible to change yourself. In time, experimenters discovered ways to change other people, animals and plants; or to borrow their genes.

Jack kissed men and women, cars and dogs, pikes and eels, falcons and eagles; he chewed grass, leaves and petals. He was a master. His reputation grew and the technique, or art, spread.

Almost every home had bathtubs or large vessels where strange creatures grew: designed pets and draft animals, biological sex machines with no more consciousness than their masters or mistresses wanted to give them, plants that cultivated themselves and kept their vicinity clean, living robots of all kinds.

The economy changed. Having money circulating was no longer important. What was important you learned after receiving the virus either directly from a multi or from a friend: to recede into semi-consciousness and dream what you wanted to be, or what you wanted to create.

§

Just like people through the ages had shown different talents or abilities – physical, intellectual, musical, emotional – there were greater and lesser talents when it came to handling DNA. Everybody could learn. But almost nobody was as skilled as Jack.

Apart from the ability itself, only one thing was important to own: land. Land that could be cultivated and give nutrition to the more and more fantastical creations which humans, now not always recognizable as humans, built with their dreams.

Feudal societies remained but changed. Many lords were overthrown when their subjects realized that another person was a more advanced dreamer and could give them more material advantages. The new rulers were often more lenient than the old, since their vivid imagination also meant strong empathy. Torture and death penalties quickly disappeared.

Society after society also joined together in groups that soon resembled the old countries. Languages still created natural borders.

Increasing empathy among rulers made wars peter out and disappear.

The world was entering a golden age.

In South America, the gaucho culture was reborn; gaudily clad gauchos on eight-legged Sleipner horses rode around the enormous herds of modified beef cattle, collecting them with lassos grown from boa constrictors, with the lightning-quick reflexes of houseflies.

Further north, in the disintegrated USA, the buffalo was back. The new buffalo were six-legged to carry more meat and were hunted with long-barreled and stinking methane rifles. In a romantic or meaninglessly redeeming gesture, many of the hunters had modified their bodies to resemble the original Native Americans. After almost five hundred years, braves once again rode after buffalo herds.

What had been called Arabia had been deserted and burned after the upheavals. After many years, Arabian princes from long forgotten dynasties had learned to modify genes and created plants that could survive both radiation and drought. The new grasses, flowers and trees dug down through the desert, both where there was sand and where the sand had melted to glass; the sand was pushed aside, the glass cracked, and persistent roots found their way down to more nourishment. After several years, the desert bloomed. Skillful manipulators sold their services to the West in exchange for minerals and nutrients. Soon white towers and cupola grew, first in oases, then in the new lands. Cliff dwellings like Petra lived again. Modified camels tirelessly carried in more minerals and proteins. Immense earthworms with sluggish group minds wriggled their way, leaving new waterways behind them. The Arabic countries lived again.

9

A couple of decades later, young Jack traveled north in his third body. He rode a biological car to the town where he'd grown up and then walked further inland.

The ice caps yet hadn't refrozen and the distance to the coast wasn't more than about twenty miles. The lands to the west lay more or less in waste. Lumbering had increased exponentially during the last horrible years and the naked hills looked like shaved heads.

Jack walked until he saw the great rapids. He hadn't seen Storforsen in more than a hundred years but the water still flowed, unconcerned about humans living and dying.

Below the rapids were burned remains of a hotel and other buildings. Now, nobody lived in the vicinity.

Young Jack took out a map showing his estate. He'd bought Storforsen and 20,000 square miles of land around it.

It had been cheap. Nobody else was interested.

On the bald slope north of the rapids, Jack measured an area of 85 square miles. Here, he would build his home. Here he would forget Rachel and create his life.

He carried a page, torn from an old book, in his inner pocket. When he unfolded the picture, it showed a steep brownish mountain side. At the foot of the mountain was a fantastic temple: three floors of straight, rectangular portals, so many that counting them was difficult, shaped rectilinear walls. A sloping ramp led up from the ground to the first floor. There was an enormous open terrace before the next ramp lead on.

The caption said: *The death temple of Queen Hatshepsut. This great building met tragic fame on November 17, 1997, when a terrorist attack killed more than 60 people here.*

The young Jack stared at the picture. His older self knew from earlier conversations that he always had loved this picture, long before he could read the caption. The picture was his only memory of his parents: it was torn from an old book that his parents had owned. The austerely beautiful marble temple, sharply outlined against the untouched mountain massif, made Jack feel a kind of wistful happiness.

The caption also symbolized the earlier age. Even temples several thousands of years old had suffered terrorist attacks, or been bombed by the US or other countries, while small conflicts grew larger, first masked as religious wars. The skirmishes were generally for the quickly disappearing oil.

This will be my symbol, young Jack told the dead land. My symbol for the new age. I will not be a feudal lord. No slaves; no one will serve me in that way.

I will make this nature bloom again. And this temple will never be bombed.

He paused and then went on.

Fifty years after the first bombing, Queen Hatshepsut's temple was annihilated in an American nuclear attack. Now, the lands west of Luxor are glass.

I hope and believe that somebody will cultivate that desert, too. One day.

I begin here.

A few hundred years later, the older Jack saw his younger counterpart ceremonially spit on the ground. His ability would make the barren lands blossom.

Hatshepsut had been a mere woman in a male dominated old Egypt, but her will had been so strong that she had managed to grasp power. Her will had built this temple.

Young Jack began doing the same. He reproduced the temple, as far as surviving texts and pictures made this possible, down to the smallest stone, the slightest ornament, the most obscure inscription.

Jack worked with his dreams. Every evening and morning he dreamed details in his temple. The bone-white portals and ramps. The potted plants in the portals, the pots for the first time in history being as alive as the plants they contained – the pots actually being parts of the plants. Statues of dazzling white enamel. Jack knew that others with his ability had created living statues, human figures that basically were plants but that gracefully moved in the wind or by their own power, but he didn't want anything like that. It felt unworthy.

He worked, he traveled, he studied. He learned everything that the old culture had known about Queen Hatshepsut, just to make his temple as like hers as was possible. One of the first biological airplanes flew him to Luxor, where he would see what was left of Hatshepsut's real temple; he rode in a cart behind a team of miniature camels across the molten glass desert to the Valley of the Queens and saw in stunning heat how the remains of the temple had flowed down into the valley; he stood in awe before the last recognizable portal.

His guide was an Untouched, a human who showed no signs at all of being modified. She was called Isis and watched Jack as he kissed the ground.

"You manipulate?" she said in halting English. "Help me?"

"How?"

"Make me healthy."

He studied her but saw no signs of disease.

"Tumor," she said. Gesticulated. "Tumor in ... place where kids grown."

Jack kissed her and dreamed.

"You want sex?" she asked after the kiss.

She was young and beautiful but she wasn't Rachel.

He shook his head.

He flew home again, eagerly reading old pamphlets that he'd bought in the sole and newly built medina in Luxor. He had paid in the same way that he removed the guide's tumor: he laid down on a lounger, in early afternoon, and waited until his thoughts became lazy and disorganized. Then, without leaving his dreams, he imagined the seller's wife, twenty years younger and seventy pounds lighter.

The overweight woman looked dubious and spoke quick Arabic before Jack kissed her and mixed his saliva with her. And the seller thankfully pressed his palms together while Jack left the place with a guide book about the Valley of the Kings, worn and visibly burned on one side but still readable. A relic from 20th century tourism.

When he came home, he resumed working on his temple. He honed details and let quickly grown parts recover.

Most of the temple was bone and enamel and didn't need much nourishment after it was grown, but some soft furniture was more alive. He needed resources to keep them living.

Young Jack worked to increase his assets. Reindeer still roamed free on the vast clear-cut areas: the lichen which were the main food of the big animals were hard to exterminate and had quickly gained footholds again. Jack worked with the reindeer, not just to modify them into riding animals and pet dolls, but also to create a new ecology.

The lichen contained many of the minerals needed to build new cells. Almost two centuries after the upheavals, Jack found himself one of the largest reindeer owners in what had been northern Sweden.

Jack kept producing, honed his dreams and their results; he built a fortune in biologic and mineral materials. He worked wholeheartedly, threw himself into his projects with something that sometimes looked like possession, both on the growing enamel and when he traveled. Everything was an attempt to forget the girl with the big eyes. Sometimes it worked, but never for long.

One hundred and thirty years and four bodies passed before the temple had risen from the earth and was finished. Jack studied his work, calm and analytic, and saw that it was good.

The next morning, he started examining other ways to use modified genes.

Many manipulators worked with telepathy, hoping to be able to unite mankind, once and for all. But telepathy didn't work.

Keeping one's memories in cultivated brains worked well. Anyone who had the resources could, in principle, keep all their memories from hundreds of years in detail, reliving day after day if they wanted to. The step to creating telepathic contact didn't seem insurmountable. First, it was a matter of letting people access each other's stored memories, then of connecting two or more people with nerve fiber, and finally of making the connection wireless.

Removing the nerve fibers was simple. Jack was one of the manipulators working with migrating birds' genes, using their ability to navigate and stay in contact as a starting point. Contact between brains was harder.

§

It probably was tried hundreds of times, in many places. Jack personally knew of about twenty experiments and supposed that there were many more.

The attempts always ended in the same way. When one person's consciousness made contact with another's, it fell apart.

The experiments were repeated over and over again, with new subjects, with new conditions, with different modifications. Nothing worked.

The self fell apart. Women and men who had volunteered as subjects quickly began speaking in disconnected ways. Confused sentences deteriorated to isolated words. At last, the subjects fell silent forever.

Their brains were analyzed, using nerve fibers, but nothing wrong was found. Everything seemed as it should be. But the self, the individual, was gone.

Nobody died. All subjects had uploaded their memories right before the experiments and lived on with just a short break in their consciousness. But the brain and body they had had during the experiment could only be used as biological material.

There were different theories. Jack believed in the theory stating that two consciousnesses in direct contact with each other immediately started a swift mirroring and feedback process. When a consciousness met its own memories nothing like that happened: all association paths where in their old well-known places, neurons knew their well-trodden tracks, everything was business as usual. But when two consciousnesses met there suddenly were new paths to choose from, new possibilities; every new choice created even more new possibilities, this happened from two directions simultaneously, and the noise of possibilities soon led to overload and collapse.

Attempts were made to not go very far down, or in, the other's self; to stay at the surface.

It didn't work. Consciousness was like a virus, quickly finding shortcuts and negotiating obstacles. The process was exponential, happening in seconds.

And the body stopped: sat unmoving, with gaping mouth and regularly blinking eyes, breathing softly, regulated and kept alive by the autonomous nervous system but no more human than an orchid or a cactus.

Consciousness, said a researcher that Jack found on the biological net, is unique for every human. We exchange our bodies, even our brains, but our consciousness is what we *really* are. Fusing this with somebody else's is impossible. As impossible as breathing in and out at the same time: the result is paradox, stop, death.

The bionet was wireless, based on insects' communication. Holos, virtuals, news, music, facts and entertainment spun the world into an enormous cocoon of information, just like before the upheavals.

Nine tenths of the still relatively small population lay on sunny beaches and received the information. Supposedly, they were happy. They ate, slept and reproduced.

The population grew.

Alone in his half-living temple, decades later, Jack still replayed his memories as holos. One day, not yet but soon, he would play a few of them virtually.

He was moving, resolute and concentrated, towards the most important event of his life.

Rachel.

10

Things were drawing to a close. Jack knew he was approaching the memories of the girl.

His imagination gave him a picture, in the same way a multi could have done: walking on a beach, toward the sea, and testing the waters with his toe.

He wanted to be careful.

After seven hundred years, Jack wanted to not only watch his memories of Rachel, but to experience them. Virtually. He wanted to be ready for them. To enjoy them. And he had to be prepared.

Most of all, he wanted to be prepared. He knew his memories ended with sadness. Sadness, tragedy, unpleasantness. Failure. Somehow.

Otherwise, why should he have traveled thirty-two light-years away from them?

He wanted to experience them. But he had to be ready.

A snapshot: alone in the sunshine on the wide terrace of enamel. His sharp shadow wandering around him while he dreamed with eyes closed. Everything sharply demarcated, well-defined.

Jack returned to his earlier memories. He didn't want to experience the later ones yet; they could contain memories of memories.

Memory is alive, a process. Like other processes, it can be recorded. The recording can be of high or low quality.

Listening to music being played live, by musicians, is not the same thing as hearing a recording. Experiencing a kiss is not the same thing as seeing it in a holo.

Remembering the memory of a kiss can be as strong as experiencing the kiss. But memories change.

A memory was a memory. For instance, the memory of a kiss. The next day, walking home in the morning. Jack remembered Liya. Walking in the morning with her kisses still lingering on his lips.

But the next time you think of a memory, there is also a memory of the memory. Consciousness turns the memory over, examines it from all directions, imagining how it *could* have been. This is necessary, since one of memory's primary functions is to prepare the mind for things that may happen: Here's a precipice; what will happen if I step out over it? I will fall. I know this without ever having taken that step; I have seen stones roll over precipices, maybe seen animals fall, I know what it is to stumble over a stone or to lose balance on a slope and feel gravity taking over. The memories of such things are added together, making me avoid the precipice.

The continuous process and interplay makes memories unreliable. And this goes especially for favorite memories, since these appear in consciousness – or semi-consciousness – more often than others. The first time he thought of kissing Liya, the memory was already colored by Shylock's cold brown morning air.

So what really happened? What was the *real* truth of the night with Rachel that Jack imagined but still didn't dare to re-experience? What was the reality behind a memory that consciousness had picked at for twenty or four hundred years, a memory that might have been retold hundreds of times – "I might have been three, it was summer, my parents were sitting in the sun in front of our house, I ran towards them, fell and grazed my knee?" Especially after the memory had been told, over and over again, until the words used had become a part of the original memory and the phrase "in the sun in front of our house" mingled the memory with hundreds of other experiences in the sun, in front of the house, in the sun in front of the house.

Jack was absolutely sure that he still had his memories of Rachel. He also supposed that he had stored them as soon as possible, before they had been garbled by contact with themselves.

He was very aware that as soon as he replayed them, virtually, to experience all physical sensations and feelings, they would become a part of his present consciousness. Even during the replay, his present thoughts and feelings would influence his experiences.

Afterwards, he would remember the recorded memory, he would remember the memory of it, and what had once been fresh and original would slowly deteriorate.

To regain the most genuine memory he could reach, he would have had to erase parts of his mind again and start over: with a fresh recorded memory, quickly changing as it met itself in Jack's consciousness.

This was a dilemma.

But he carried on. He played more memories from his time at Matti's farm, just as holos; he didn't need or want to make them virtual yet; he could tell from his own reactions, his eyes watching for Rachel or following her when they'd found her, how he gradually got infatuated with the girl.

This was at a distance and it was hopeless. But Jack wasn't going to let small problems like hopelessness stop him.

No more than any other infatuated human being would have done.

Young Jack must have tried to find a way to make contact with her. His older self gathered this from his younger self's way of sitting in his room, by now a room that he had to himself, staring at the wall for several minutes. And then quickly rising, walking around in the room, seemingly full of new energy; sometimes he sat down again, eyes lowered, as if he had discovered some problem with his plan; at other times he rushed out, ran through the woods or did something else to release his energy.

The older Jack saw his younger self running through whipping trees, heard the gasping breaths and the footsteps thumping on the soft ground.

He couldn't tell if he was happy.

Jack fast-forwarded the long working days and concentrated on mornings, lunches and evenings; the times when he might have seen Rachel.

Seeing her often made him sad. Every day she spoke to the young noblemen on the farm. Sometimes the conversations were long and intimate. Sometimes she walked away with one of them and Jack was tortured by his younger self not daring to follow, not knowing what was happening. Sometimes the young Jack went to bed; other times he waited up, listlessly talking with the other farmhands, until most of them had yawned and gone to bed and he seemed to realize it would seem strange if he stayed alone.

Of course, young Jack didn't know what happened when she went with other young men. He must have guessed, his imagination building pictures that he tried to free himself from; but this didn't seem to interfere with his infatuation. This appeared to keep growing, irrespective of whether it was fertilized with hope or with despair.

The boy kept close to her. Discreetly, of course, very discreetly, he didn't want the feudal lord's daughter to think he was stalking her. But he kept close. A couple of times, the older Jack thought, the boy was close to carrying out one of his plans: during a feast night, he might get some food or drink and serve Rachel; on a summer morning, he might be ready with horse and carriage if she wanted to go somewhere. It seemed as if he did try. But his plans never succeeded. He never got a chance to talk to her.

She was the one who contacted him.

She came during his second summer at the farm, after the mild and short winter. The month was May and it was already hot enough to burn the grass brown if it didn't rain for a couple of days.

Jack was standing watering a garden patch when he reacted to a sound behind him. He turned and saw Rachel.

"Hi," she said. He mumbled something in confusion.

This must have been the moment he'd been imagining for more than a year, the moment he had dreamed of in every waking moment. Except right now. No doubt, he had prepared hundreds of funny and touching and wise things to say; he must have been lying in his bed, night after night, concocting ingenious answers for whatever Rachel would say if she finally, some day, spoke to him.

Now, she said "Hi," and he didn't seem to have an answer.

"You're Jack, right?" she said. "Isn't that your name?"

"Yes," he got out.

She said, "We're going to play racquetball. Jenny and me and Max and Love. You know the game?"

"Racquets," he said. "Net. Balls?"

She suddenly smiled, and even seven hundred years later Jack's breast filled with something indescribable.

"Can you say more than single words?" she said.

He said, "Yes."

He couldn't have meant that as a joke but she laughed anyway. Her laugh must have filled him with even more feelings, but also have given him time to draw a deep breath and land in himself again. She told him that she and her friends wanted help setting up the net, and Jack took care of this as quickly and efficiently as he could. When he was done and the four youngsters went out on the court in their white clothes Jack lingered; Rachel asked him what he wanted and he said that he just wanted to check that the net was properly set.

Her eyes were big and dark. He could see her body move under her clothes. And when he left, she smiled and waved to him.

She even said "Thank you."

Since that day, she knew who he was.

He had to stop the playback. Somehow, in some unfathomable way, he knew it was getting closer.

Must be my unconscious, he thought. As Liya said of her memories from childhood. In some way they remain, the most important parts remain, even if you empty your brain of memories. The essential things are what make you be you – they are not only what is in your mind, they are what shaped your mind. They come back.

The older Jack made himself take a break. He did other things for a couple of days; examined plants and living materials, rejuvenated cells here and there, changed plants that were irreversibly aged; he took long walks, saw the water streaming in the ancient rapids, saw the sun set behind the temple and the white airfield he had created.

One evening, he studied the clumps of brain tissue and wondered how many times this had happened before. How many times he had buried his memories, maybe traveled to other planets; how many times his subconscious had drawn him to somebody who looked like Rachel.

And thrown them away because they weren't her.

11

He prepared carefully. Waited for the right moment, without having any idea of when it would come. He was sure his subconscious would lead him.

After two weeks, he felt that the time had come. He ate a carefully calculated and balanced meal before he slowly and somehow solemnly walked into the chamber where the semicircle of brains waited for him.

He preferred nerve fiber to wireless. Nerve fiber felt more reliable.

A river of memories and impressions washed over him. This always happened during the first seconds: memory was holographic in time and space and needed a moment before you found what you wanted and could play it sequentially.

This time was worse than ever. He replayed his memories virtually with all impressions and thoughts and feelings. Both his present self and the self that had experienced this several hundred years ago were highly emotionally charged. When all the feelings collided, feedback loops came into being, not unlike the ones that had caused catastrophes during experiments with telepathy.

Jack swallowed and closed his eyes; closing his eyes was meaningless, since the confusion was within him, but his reflexes took charge.

After a few seconds, nausea subsided and he found what he was looking for.

It was late summer, no doubt the same year as the memories he'd watched lately. Rachel and everybody else looked the same, as did the farm itself. Everybody living at the farm, nobility as well as workers, sat at a long table between the houses, eating and drinking. A kind of harvest festival.

The month was early October, but it was as hot as August had been before the upheavals.

Even after the nausea had subsided, the older Jack was overwhelmed by his younger self's feelings.

The boy was possessed. There was no other word.

Young Jack was continually aware of where Rachel was. He sat with his fellow workers, more or less maintaining a conversation with them. But his soul was somewhere else.

The boy also kept a continuous inner monologue, ragged fragments, halfway articulated, about his hopes and his despair: now Rachel was speaking to Jenny and everything was fine; now she turned to Max and smiled to him. And panic grew.

The older Jack felt a strange nostalgia about being so young and experiencing such violent emotions. He immediately took this back. Weren't his feelings quite as violent now? Hadn't he traveled sixty-four light-years, first to leave the dark-eyed girl behind and then to find her again?

But still. There was a naiveté or originality in the boy's desperation. A feeling of *I want this now!* that was more direct, more childishly urgent, than what Jack felt now.

Seven centuries of experience separate me from him, he thought. The years have left their mark.

The evening on Matti's farm was dark and warm. A few hours had passed. Young Jack was still in turmoil, still furtively glancing at the head table where Rachel and her friends sat. He didn't seem to notice that a girl at his own table gradually moved closer to him; at last, when the party was already drawing to a close, she was sitting next to Jack, trying to talk to him. Her name was Anna.

"Nice evening," she said, trying to hide her uncertainty.

The older Jack was buried deep within his younger self. He could see how attractive this girl was, and how attracted she was to the younger Jack. He also thought that he was more aware of what Anna wanted than young Jack was.

"Yes," the boy said, glancing at the head table.

"You think she is beautiful?"

The words needed a moment to sink in. "Who?" he said.

"Rachel."

"Rachel? Oh, her." He shrugged. "Sure."

"You like dark-haired girls?"

He looked at Anna, really saw her, for the first time. Dark hair, big mouth, straight but maybe just a tad long nose. Slim and strong under her coarse overalls. A little shorter than Rachel.

"Yes," he said. "No. I don't know." The situation was hopeless: if he liked dark girls the next question would of course be if he liked her, Anna, since she was dark; if he said he didn't he would be rude. And furthermore, any answer might provoke more questions about Rachel.

"You don't know?" She laughed, more confident than before.

"It's hard to say. It's like asking if you prefer food or drink."

"I prefer drink," she said, serving herself more rowanberry wine. "You want some?"

"No, thanks. Yes, sure," he changed his mind. She immediately filled his glass.

"You seem a little indecisive," she said. "Are you a Pisces?"

"Pisces?" he echoed in confusion.

Rachel was in an intense conversation with Max right now, heads close together. Jack tried to maintain his eye contact with Anna just enough: not being rude, not making her ask what he was looking at. But at the same time not being too open and accessible.

Not to give her any hope.

How young he is, older Jack thought in the blast of emotional hurricanes. So very young and so hopelessly obsessed with something he can't have.

But that he will have.

Or ...?

Suddenly, he was unsure. All his memories, everything he had found, told him that he was and always had been obsessed with Rachel. But did this mean that he ever had been with her?

Maybe it was just an unfulfilled dream.

The thought frightened him, and his fear surprised him. What did it matter? Rachel also was hundreds of years older by now. She could be dead; she could be married, she might have emigrated to some colony planet. Or whatever. He had to be able to break free of her. And in that case, wouldn't it have been better if he had never kissed her, never slept with her?

All of older Jack's subconscious rebelled at that thought. He imagined how all the quintillion particles in the multiverse, straying every which way a moment ago – how these particles united, as iron filings shape patterns by a magnet, and strived in the same direction.

Towards Rachel.

He was agitated. But he couldn't leave his memories.

"Pisces," Anna said. "The star sign. February to March?"

"Oh, astrology. No, I was born on April twenty."

"I see. Aries on the verge of Taurus." She seemed a little disappointed. "I'm a Scorpio. Scorpio and Pisces are a fantastic combination in bed."

Rachel's and Max' heads were even closer together now. Jack had no idea of what to say to Anna. He was nervous about this astrology angle – suddenly, she might remember that the ascendant in his sign, or the moon's phase, made them a perfect couple this very night.

"Hm," he said.

That worked. She was silent for a moment.

Before Anna left, she served him more wine. It was suddenly much later and most had gone to bed. Even the head table was less crowded.

"It was nice talking to you," Anna said in a tone that didn't match her words.

"Hm," he said, well aware that he was being rude. But this seemed to work.

She stood there for a moment, pitcher in hand. He knew he ought to say something but had no idea what. His thoughts were elsewhere.

"Well. Good night, then."

"Good night."

He didn't even look up.

Jack was alone at his table, excepting a couple that from all appearances already had begun their foreplay. They didn't see him. He didn't see them, either.

Rachel got to her feet, a little wobbly. She helped an even wobblier Max to stand.

And led him away.

Panic.

He sat there, suddenly more aware of small groans and other sounds from the couple on the other side of the table. Rachel and Max disappeared behind the corner of the main building.

The worst of it all was that Rachel turned right at the corner.

She looked straight at Jack. He immediately stared down into the table. But she had seen his glance.

The loving couple at his table managed to stand up and staggered towards one of the workers' houses, supporting each other or almost falling together. They tittered loudly and shushed each other. A few people were still at the tables and nobody could miss the inebriated lovers.

Jack was alone at his table. He waited.

No Rachel.

He didn't want to imagine what she was doing but couldn't help it. Pictures raced through his head. Rachel and Max. Max and Rachel. The pictures mixed with the tipsy couple that had just left and it all became unbearable.

He had to go. He couldn't sit here alone, staring at nothing.

Soon. He would go very soon.

He just had a little wine left.

He drank slowly, swirling the wine in his glass, pretended to thoughtfully and philosophically look out at the almost deserted yard. Outwardly calm, chaotic within.

Finally, even the dregs were irretrievably finished and he had to go. That hurt.

His room was on the far side of the smaller workers' building.

"Jack."

He heard the whisper and looked at the dark pine forest. At first, he didn't see her – she had pulled on a black cape.

"Jack!"

She waited at the edge of the woods, a few yards away.

He immediately knew.

The older Jack reclined, eyes closed, with the nerve fiber below his ear; he might have been asleep. Or dead. But he was alive.

Seven centuries had passed since he felt this alive.

"Max?" she said, whispering. They were in Jack's room and didn't want to wake anybody up. She tittered. "Max? That drunk. I just had to help him to bed."

"But –" He didn't know how to continue.

"Why you?" She ran a nail along his forearm and his entire body shuddered. "I've seen you looking at me. And I couldn't avoid seeing you, either."

It was too good to be true. Still, it was happening.

The older Jack relived that night in every detail, well aware that these memories would be distorted next time he thought about them. His soul big-eyed, he noted every caress, every kiss; every soft down on Rachel's body; every glance, every muted moan and helpless sigh. Her eyes and mouth captured him over and over again, always in new ways. He marveled at every moment, at feeling her weight on top of him, at having her captured under him. He marveled at the raging storms and the calm between them, at the whispers, at the soft caresses, always turning to something else when the shudders shook their bodies.

Nothing in his life could compare to this. Neither sooner or later. Not Liya, nor any other woman. Waves came and subsided, pushing Jack and Rachel in front of them, throwing them in deep valleys and hurling them up to foaming peaks. Both were sleek with sweat, got cold and hid under the comforter; then heat rose and they threw the bedclothes off again.

Nothing else could match this. Nothing in the entire multiverse.

God, the older Jack thought several hours later. I understand myself. Why I've been possessed. I had an impossible dream and it became true.

His younger self was lying with eyes open, Rachel sleepily twirling his chest hairs. He was well aware that a day of hard work waited and that he hadn't slept a single moment, but this didn't bother him at all.

It was worth it.

Neither of the two had ever felt anything like this. Joy filled the younger Jack's being, filled his soul, and radiated into the older man: sometimes the younger man felt like he had left his own body and was watching himself from a distance, momentarily thinking that this was a dream. But it was no dream.

Rachel sneaked away minutes before dawn, wrapped in the black cape, hood over her head.

"Thank you," she whispered when she kissed him one last time. She was leaning over him; he lay naked in bed.

"See you."

She smiled, teasing him by pulling the comforter over his eyes. Then she was gone.

While the younger Jack waited for daybreak, his imagination built impossible dreams of their life together. He would marry Rachel. He would inherit this farm.

Matti would give Jack and Rachel part of his land.

Rachel and Jack would elope together. They would make their way to Oresund and build a new life in the South.

He smiled, drowsily.

Young Jack thought about showering but wanted to remember Rachel on his body. He dressed in clean overalls and went out to work.

The sun was August hot and he was impossibly tired. It was the best morning of his life.

At lunchtime, the supervisor came and wanted to speak to Jack. Jack followed him to his small office.

"You're not needed anymore," the supervisor said curtly. His name was Harald. He was a couple of years past fifty, with a stout and strong body. His hair had turned white years ago.

Jack's jaws worked. "What?"

"We need less people during winter. Matti decided that you and three others have to go."

"Who else?"

"Never mind that. Pack your stuff. Be out of here before dinner."

Jack desperately looked for Rachel. She wasn't to be seen.

He couldn't go into the main building without a pretext. And there was nobody he could send a message by.

Anna, the girl from last evening, was the only one who said good-bye.

He walked south, trying to understand what had happened.

Her parents must have heard, he thought. Maybe Max had become jealous. Waked up in the night, gone to Rachel's room and not found her. He could have waited there, or outside, until she came back in the morning.

Or maybe her mother. Or her father.

His throat constricted when he thought of Rachel. Did she know what had happened? Would she think Jack had left because of some misunderstanding?

Jack stopped. The autumn woods were hot. Needles and shrubs were partly brown, desiccated.

He had to go back.

He was almost back at the farm when he suddenly stopped.

What would happen to Rachel if he turned up at her home again?

Pictures rushed by. He didn't like any of them.

Crying, he went south again.

The older Jack was ready to drop with fatigue when he stood up. Seen from outside, he'd been sitting immovable for eleven hours. Within himself, he had relived the worst emotional storms in his life.

§

Jack hadn't stopped at his younger self's sorrowful trek away from the farm and Rachel. He'd made a few spot tests after that. He'd seen the younger Jack writing letters. He'd also seen his younger self walk almost all the way to the farm still another time, but immediately being chased away by the supervisor and some workers.

Tossing and turning in sheets whose dampness wasn't lovely at all, but suffocating, nasty.

At last, he'd reached memories that he'd already seen. He saw the multi give him the virus, making him ready to modify genes. That was when he disconnected the nerve fiber and stood on shaky feet.

A couple of days went by while the older Jack tried to compose himself. He belatedly realized that he had had an unspoken plan of trying to break free of Rachel by reliving his memories.

It hadn't worked.

A message came over the bionet, from Liya. She still was on the inhospitable planet. However, they worked diligently and the colony became more tolerable by the year. She missed Jack, as a friend.

She was in a relationship with a Canadian man and hoped to get pregnant soon. She hoped Jack was well and promised to get in touch again.

The message had been sent thirty-two years ago: forty-one years after Jack had left the planet.

I was dead then, Jack thought. My genome was rushing through space, waiting to build a new body. While Liya's radio signals chased me.

He wondered if Liya had built a new body. Small and slim.

She had contacted him after twelve of her short years. He hoped she didn't miss him more than she admitted.

He wondered how many times before he had done this; or similar things. Hidden his memories, tried to break free. And got stuck again. Drowning in Rachel's eyes.

This may be the fifth time, he thought while the bioplane descended to Rio de Janeiro. I may have contacted her five or ten times before, been disappointed by her, hidden my memories; created new bodies; traveled to some colony or to a new part of Earth.

I may have erased more memories than I have left.

But not been able to destroy that night.

He closed his eyes, dreaming of the night seven hundred years ago.

It had taken him more than a week, but at last he'd found her on the net. Her name now was Rachel Murilo Resende and she lived in one of the slopes above Copacabana. The house was beautiful, grown from white enamel just as Jack's own temple. Jack was met by a maid whose black-and-white uniform obviously was a part of herself.

This disturbed him. He didn't like biological servant robots.

Rachel was alone. She waited for him in a big and sunlit room, facing the sea.

She was gaunt, almost a skeleton, and greedily ate a grilled chicken. He could see bones working under the skin of her hands.

"Isn't it great?" she said when she caught him looking. "I did the modifications myself. Better this than looking like a cat, I always say. Of course, I have to go to the loo all the time." Her laugh was just a tad forced as she bit into the chicken again.

This was Rachel. The dream of his life. He stood before her, looking into her eyes.

Her eyes were the worst. Rachel couldn't weigh more than ninety pounds. Why had she chosen to modify her genes in this way? Didn't she care about her sharp pelvis, clearly visible when she turned, still chewing?

He could stand the skeleton-like body. It wasn't lovely, but he could stand it. Or rather, he would have been able to stand it if her eyes, now sunken below her forehead, had been exactly as they were then. Except for one small detail.

Her eyes missed the tenderness they had had that night.

They sat and Jack told her a slightly edited version of his memories. Without mentioning their night together.

No gleam of recognition lit her eyes.

"No," she said, munching a piece of honey cake with melted chocolate. "Sorry. I remember the farm, of course, my parents and living on that farm. I remember Max and Love ... But not you. What did you say you worked with?"

He told her of his work as a foreman. Building, harvesting, chopping firewood. She nodded, still without recognition.

"There were a lot of people there," she said. She wistfully looked at the honey cake, hesitated for a moment and grabbed another piece. "I can't remember everybody ..."

"And I've never been to see you before? I mean, later?"

She shrugged. "Can't tell. This is my what, twentieth body? Twenty-third? I'm sorry but I only keep ... important ... memories with me. You know?"

He decided to be polite and civil.

"Have you lived here long?"

She thought. "About fifty years. Since I met Gabriel. My husband."

"What does he do?"

Rachel waved a bony hand. "He produces virtuals. You know. Never-ending love and all that."

Her laughter was shrill and Jack suddenly had to leave.

Flying home, he once again dreamed of his night with Rachel. But in the middle of the night, in the middle of his most precious memory, she turned into the living skeleton he'd just met.

He woke in panic.

Jack didn't know what to do. Days and weeks passed while he wandered in the searing sun outside his temple or sat on the bank, letting himself be hypnotized by the roar of the rapids.

He replayed his memories once again, just watching. And once more, a few days later.

Both times left him exhausted and sad.

A part of him wanted to replay the memories over and over, allow himself to disappear into them. But that would mean giving up. Jack didn't want to give up. Not yet.

The young man buried himself in work. He designed new connections for the bionet and new and faster nerve fibers. After that, he worked with space travel for some months.

Jack's name began appearing on the net. Now and then he was visited by old friends and old girlfriends; he remembered some of them; most weren't in his present memories, possibly because he had been obsessed by Rachel when he knew them and they had disappeared when he erased everything connected with her.

Something that hadn't done him much good.

He quickly dispatched the guests. He preferred being along and dreaming of Rachel.

He spent more and more time in hypnagogic states. It didn't take him very long to learn how to float between dream and reality for hours. He liked that experience. He was the overlord of his own universe, floating like a fetus in his slow dreams.

§

Rachel was always there. After all, it was his own universe.

Once again, he felt himself growing obsessed. Maybe he had been so already on Shylock, even when Liya's eyes filled him with a longing that he couldn't understand; but at that time, he'd held back, hesitated, been unsure.

Now he knew. Now he let his obsession take over him, break into every cell, every thought, every dream. The dream was impossible but he would never give up. He would find her, somewhere; she filled his universe. She *was* his universe.

He suddenly opened his eyes. Autumn was closing in on the Northern tundra and the sun wasn't as high in the sky anymore.

His universe.

Jack stood up. He wanted to talk to a multi.

12

He didn't have to wait very long. The next time he descended into waking dreams, the sunlight seemed to change. Jack opened his eyes and saw the blurred shape materialize in front of him.

It was a beautiful September day. Jack had planted trees below the temple and the rapids, conifer and birch, to make the dry ground live again. So far, he didn't need the land above. Up there, the ground was still more or less naked, except for lichen. But below the temple were green sprouts.

I have created this, Jack thought. By dreaming.

The multi swirled in front of him and Jack saw an enormous and fuzzy question mark in front of him.

Jack told the multi of his life. His obsession with Rachel. Shylock and his other attempts to break free.

He told it of the Rachel he had met in Rio.

Then he asked about the multiverse.

He said, "If I have this right, the multiverse is the set of all possible variants of our universe. And in that case." He hesitated, looking for words, but knew that the multi had already seen his thoughts. "In that case, the Rachel I want can be found somewhere."

He paused again.

"Am I right?"

Jack could understand the multi better now. They had developed a repertoire of pictures, a kind of language. Their communication seemed to become more and more like a normal conversation.

The multi's pictures showed Jack that it was possible to find another Rachel. But there was a catch.

It would cost him. Time and work.

"Teach me," Jack said.

The multi taught him. It showed Jack the familiar double-slit experiment: single photons passing double slits and strangely appearing as wave patterns. One interpretation of this was that the wave patterns were created by the photons interfering with other particles – but since there were only single photons in the experiments, they had to be interfering with their counterparts in other universes, other photons. Around the year 2000, several theories of the multiverse had appeared, the concept gradually being accepted.

But the ramifications were stunning.

The multi went on. Jack saw himself, standing on the highest enamel terrace of his temple, at this moment, next to the multi.

The picture split into two identical ones. Again and again. Jack soon lost count. An endless sequence of pictures showing himself and the multi, standing facing each other, quickly raced through his mind.

The tempo increased. The pictures changed. Picture after picture blurred by: Jack standing, sitting, lying down; Jack troubled, smiling, crying in despair or happily laughing.

Everything was happening somewhere, right now, in different universes.

Every state a particle could be in meant a new universe. Thus the total number of universes was many times greater than the number of particles in one universe, including photons and dark matter, raised to the power of itself.

This wasn't infinity, not mathematically speaking. But to humans, the number of logically possible universes was for all practical purposes more than infinite.

Jack asked the multi what it meant by logically possible universes.

The multi showed him. Jack saw himself standing outside the temple, in thousands of editions; he saw the meteoroid coming, a quick light across the darkening sky, invisible in one moment, then filling all the world. He saw every possible variant of his and Rachel's one night together, scattered over what he thought was at least a couple of hundred years; once again, he saw the night or nights ending happily or in despair, with him and Rachel together or not, at all possible times and in all conceivable situations, in his room, in the woods, in the yard, in a closet, in the kitchen of the main building, on the steps of the palace-like main building, on the green grass of a ditch, in the wistful silence of Rachel's room; he saw, since this was possible, exactly the same scenes and millions of variations played out with the other girl, Anna, the girl whom he hadn't wanted just because she wasn't Rachel; he saw himself during a night with that girl, in her room, in his room and in thousands of other places; he saw her cry or laugh when he left her, saw himself smile and shrug, or opening his veins, when Anna left him in the morning. He saw his time with Liya on the bare colony planet fork in the same way: Liya wanted children, he himself wanted children, Liya left him for Veen, Jack left Liya for Sara and for Veen and for Peter; Jack and Veen and Liya lived as a triad; Jack became the only one staying on Shylock, alone under dark clouds with cold waves whipping the shore, as everybody else gave up and went back to Earth.

The theoretical number of nucleic acids in DNA, Jack had heard centuries ago, was ten to the power of one hundred and twenty thousand. He couldn't even imagine a number that would hold the set of possible universes, meaning every possible state and position for every particle in every Planck time, in every universe. Googolplex, he thought, 1 followed by a googol of zeroes: googolplex raised to the power of googolplex.

Everything Jack had seen was logically possible. And due to the structure of the multiverse, where every situation containing several possibilities meant that both or all possibilities became real in some universe, it had happened or should happen.

Jack couldn't break the laws of logic. He couldn't be dead and alive at the same time and in the same universe. In just one universe, he couldn't be both Jack and Veen. But in the multiverse, this changed. In just one universe, he couldn't both find his Rachel and not. But in the multiverse it was logically possible that Jack, or millions of copies of him, would find the one Rachel he was looking for.

And so it had to happen, in innumerable universes. And that he would have to search in the set of everything possible, in the totality of everything existing; in the universe, raised to the power of all its possibilities.

Jack was getting impatient but the multi showed him one more thing.

Jack saw himself and Rachel walking across the enamel in thousands of editions, like thousands of moving pictures placed behind each other, a little askance, so that Jack could see parts of almost all the pictures.

The image in his head zoomed in on a few of the pictures. They were very close to one another, five or six copies where Rachel smiled at him. Rachel in the middle picture disappeared and Jack was left alone. In the other pictures, she still smiled at him.

The pictures began to blur and melt into each other. There was still no Rachel in the middle picture, but the two pictures at each side mixed with the middle one, floated into it, until a kind of shadow appeared where the girl had been.

At last, Jack understood. His impatience vanished and he breathed in, almost gasped, just once.

"You mean," he said, "that all dreams and fantasies are caused by interference? Interference between universes?"

Not all, the multi told him. But many.

Jack thought. "Every time you worry that something will happen, or long for something – it's interference? Not just my memories of Rachel? All thoughts and images, everything happening in my mind, all hope and fear – all can be related to things happening in other universes? And the particles constituting my brain and creating my mind also interfere with their counterparts in other universes?"

Not quite all thoughts, the multi said. But many.

"I see," Jack slowly said. "Why should only photons interact? Why not all kinds of particles? This explains a lot. On Shylock, when I dreamed of her ... that wasn't just my subconscious. It was leakage from other worlds."

He thought while images slid past.

"And everything I dream," he said. "It's really happening? For real. Somewhere, in some other universe? My dreams are real?"

The multi confirmed.

Jack and Rachel kissed. The kiss was tender and soft and seemed never to end.

"It's happening somewhere," Jack said. "Right now." He thought. Then he spoke, faster and faster, becoming more and more agitated. "Rachel and I are happy together. Another Rachel, not the one I met in Rio. The one I'm dreaming of. My Rachel. She is somewhere. Millions of copies, in billions of universes. And in many of these I must have emigrated, or died. Rachel is there, alone, the Rachel I'm dreaming of. She has to be. My dreams are interference. And she's dreaming of me. Somewhere. She has to be, since I'm hoping for her to do it and my dreams are interference ...

"She's dreaming of me."

He checked himself. Watched the multi, threw his hands out. "And your race knows how to travel between universes."

The shimmering creature bowed.

"Teach me."

13

Again, Jack worked. The work appealed to him. All his life, he thought, had been made up from such projects, situations where he was working towards a goal. Winning Rachel may have been the first; then manipulating genes; with time, the attempts to free himself of Rachel, culminating in his voyage to Shylock; and now this.

He didn't know if he should be thankful for his projects. Maybe it would have been better for him to lie at a pool in New Zealand, dedicating himself to sex and virtuals, never interpreting the word "dreams" as something besides the frolics his brain was up to when he slept.

Maybe it even would be better, he thought, to live on a mountain in Rio, devoting myself to food.

But he couldn't choose. He was who he was and he had to make another attempt. Another attempt to find the Rachel in his dreams. The version he wanted, somewhere in the multiverse.

The process was similar to modifying genes. He had to dream about something, put himself in a state where his dreams seemed real. And at last catch them.

Turn them into reality.

One of the childhood memories that Jack now carried again was about his father, showing him that very thing: how dreams could change reality. The conversation had taken place long before human beings tried to modify their genes, long before anybody knew about multis, even before the upheavals.

Maybe Jack's father had told him because his son, even as a child, had been a dreamer. Or maybe Jack had become a dreamer partly because of what his father taught him.

They were in the old house with the enormous ceiling height that Magnus, Jack's father, had built many years ago. Jack couldn't have been more then four or five years old. The memory was no doubt distorted, colored by all the times he had thought about it, mixing it up with similar situations. But that didn't matter. The essence was there.

"Look around you," Magnus said. Jack sat in the gray sofa, looking up to the ceiling. The house resembled a church with its high and slim windows. The feeling of space.

"Look around," Magnus said again. "Look at the walls. The ceiling and the floor. The windows. The lamps and furniture and pictures. The books."

Magnus had thousands of books, inherited from his parents. Jack looked at them, the colorful or faded backs, the letters that were still unknown to him, but that he knew could contain all the world.

"What do they have in common?" Magnus asked.

At first, Jack didn't know.

"They're made by people," he said at last.

Magnus nodded. "True. But before that?"

That nut was too hard for Jack to crack.

"Somebody thought about them," Magnus said. "Before the pictures and the books and everything else existed, somebody imagined them. One person saw a painting or a table, another imagined a book that she wanted to write. And when they'd dreamed or thought long enough, they made their dream real.

"That's what separates us from animals, Jack. We create our own world. We change the world to resemble our dreams. The Egyptian queen did it, building that temple. You will do it. And sometimes it happens almost at once. A composer may wake up with a new song in his head. Scientists and writers might solve problems in their dreams."

Seven centuries later, Jack realized that the dreams his father had talked about also could be seen as interference or leakage from other universes. In one universe was a painting; somebody, maybe the artist himself, looked at it; particles whirled in her brain. And interference created similar pictures in other brains, in other universes.

This was a paradox. Jack remembered a holo he'd seen later in his childhood. A time traveler visited 16th century London, meeting a hopeful writer named Shakespeare. The time traveler gave the writer a few of the Shakespeare plays he carried with him from his own time and thanks to that gift, the young writer was a success. Who had actually created the plays?

The paradox was unsolvable. Unless you considered the multiverse.

In the multiverse, a time traveler might very well go back, carrying a handy pocket edition of Shakespeare's plays, meeting a William Shakespeare who hadn't written these.

But the time traveler wasn't in the universe where Shakespeare already had written those plays.

According to theory, the multiverse consisted of an enormous number of snapshots or moments. These snapshots existed side by side, both in space and time. In the year 1592, there were billions of snapshots in which a William Shakespeare already had seen his first plays performed; in as many worlds, or many, many more, there was a Shakespeare with dreams, but who hadn't yet managed to write something, or to put something on the stage. When the visitor traveled in time he also traveled between universes, since every moment, every possible snapshot, was a special case of how all particles were organized.

In that view, there was no paradox. The time traveler simply brought something from his own universe to a world where it hadn't existed before.

All such thoughts also had started out as dreams. Inventions by dreaming scientists or writers.

Jack had read many such dreams as a child.

He might become the first to make them real. Just like the seed of a painting with a certain subject, the first Last Supper or La Primavera, had been dreamed up in some universe, the interference then spreading the dream, like a virus, to innumerable worlds – just like that, Jack might be the one to give humans the freedom the multis had: the freedom to travel between worlds.

He wasn't very interested in that aspect. He knew that he was a master dreamer, but he only wanted to use his gift for one purpose.

He only cared about Rachel.

§

He dreamed. Day after day, he wore himself out by long walks on the tundra above the temple or in the growing forest below. He stopped at the rapids to rest, standing on rocks that had been lying immovable before humans came here for the first time, stared into the water until his self faded away and he became one with the chaotic waves. He walked on, let his self slowly disappear again, turning into an animal in an eternal now where time didn't exist and the surrounding world was a single *here*, changing around him without him being aware that he was moving.

His hope was up. When multis appeared on Earth, he had been one of the first they'd contacted. His dreaming personality was perfectly suited to modify DNA, first his own, then that of others. Since the multi had explained to him what he should do to visit other universes, he knew that it was possible.

The authors he had read as a child had had their dreams, he thought one day, when the autumn sun at last was cooling and the quickly growing birches below the rapids burned in yellow and orange. He had read their dreams. Now, he was elevating the dreams onto levels that he couldn't remember ever seeing in their books.

That in itself was also a kind of interference. The dreams he read had poked the neurons and clusters in his brain, made him open to such ideas.

He was passing the torch.

At night, he slept deeply, tired after his long walks. He dreamed of Rachel and of Liya. Sometimes the two melted together and he didn't know who was who.

He realized that there were worlds where Liya was the one he had loved throughout his life and Rachel the one he had let down.

But those worlds weren't his own.

When he awoke he lay still, clutching sleep as long as he could, trying to hang on to his dreams of Rachel.

This was no waste of time. It would gradually bring him closer to her.

In time, tendencies appeared. Moments. A few of the first moments may have been dreams where Liya had taken Rachel's place; he couldn't know. But small things happened from time to time.

His imagination was very rich – which was what made this possible for him in the first place – and sometimes he couldn't tell it from reality.

He stood below the rapids, hearing the water roar far above. It was an October evening, a cooler October in this century, but just the season of his night with Rachel. The light and the air told him this, far below his consciousness, while the sun went down: this was how he had been, this was how the world had been, when both he and the world had been young.

He closed his eyes and let memories seep in, drowning in them. Her lip on his nipple. Her hair over his legs. The softest thing in the world. And all along, whatever he allowed himself to remember, above and beyond everything else, her eyes; the joy in her eyes.

It's all real, he thought, half dreaming. It's real in some universe, because it's possible. I have loved Rachel for hundreds of years in other worlds; I have loved Liya in others; other women and men in still other worlds. For my copies in those worlds, it's real.

He wondered how many of his versions were trying to do just what he was doing, right now. Trying to find Rachel or somebody else.

The next day, or a few weeks later – the first snow had fallen, it must have been late November or early December, but Jack had lost count of the days – he saw a vision of a world where he met Rachel.

She was all he had dreamed.

She invitingly reached her slim arms out to him; she was exactly the dream he had wanted for seven centuries; she didn't have to speak for him to know that she had wanted him for all these years. They were somewhere, he didn't know where, there were details behind her and beside her but he never saw them.

He only had eyes for her.

He took two steps towards her. But, as often in dreams, it was like moving in water. Or rather, it was as if an enormous rubber band tried to hold him back. Jack fought against it, but the band tugged at him; he saw Rachel's face turn worried when he couldn't come closer. All his strength was not enough.

He gave in and the rubber band tore him away from her.

Jack decided that the vision had been real. It had felt that way.

He wondered how she might have experienced it: that real Rachel, in her only and, for her, real world. Suddenly the love of her youth, the man she had dreamed of for hundreds of years, had appeared before her. Fought to come closer but failed.

She must have imagined it a dream. Maybe she worried about her reason. No, Jack decided; in certain universes she worried about her reason, but in others she shook it off as a meaningless hallucination or just as fantasies that she had given free rein.

But it had happened. If not in his own universe, it had happened close enough that the interference had made it feel real to him.

In time, he would succeed. If he didn't give up.

It happened again. And again.

The rubber band tore and tugged at him. Sometimes he managed to hold on for a few seconds, especially those times when he was close to Rachel: it was as if the tenderness in her eyes, her longing to have him stay, helped him to hold on for another couple of moments.

Sometimes he was immediately thrown back. Often, he had no idea what he was seeing.

Some Earths were empty, a few of them seemed to have no atmosphere: he felt a terrible pressure building in his chest and head, helplessly burped out the air in his lungs and stomach, immediately let go, was thrown back and gasped in shock. Other times he was in the middle of dense forests or great deserts, and it happened that he found himself thrashing in giant sea waves and returned sopping wet. He didn't understand.

He called for the multi.

This, too, was getting easier. The multi had taught him to use his dreams, and he called the multi by dreaming of it. Everything was connected.

The multi explained by blurred and shimmering pictures. Jack understood that the problem was about several things. It was both of his own mindset in the moment when his own will became stronger than the force that kept him in his own world, and about genes.

Jack had already changed his own body, as well as those of others, many times: to manage gravity on Shylock, because an Egyptian man wanted a younger wife, to simply live longer. The worlds most easy for Jack to reach were those where genes had chosen the same paths as in his own world.

"But the empty ones? The ones without atmosphere?"

The multi showed him. Life had been exterminated in many worlds. War and natural disasters. A solar flare could cook all biological material on a planet in minutes. Comets and asteroids could tear away the atmosphere.

And this was happening now, the multi showed him. Even in worlds where DNA had followed almost exactly the same paths as on Earth. It was happening right now, in vast sections of the multiverse. The Earth burned or froze. Humanity was extinct before believers even had time to kneel and pray.

Often there were colonies, wondering why their home planet had fallen silent.

Winter sneaked in. Snow was a thin white blanket over the tundra and the reborn forest. One night Jack wandered out, far below the temple, and looked up to the sky. Beside the temple, the rapids roared; above and below the rapids, the river was already covered with ice. The moon made a comma above the giant signs Jack had written in nature, and the stars shone brighter than he could remember ever seeing them.

He thought that the stars also were signs. Or rather, complicated dreams, put together by innumerable billions of signs, quarks and superstrings and other building blocks of matter. Below the stars was he himself: built by even more complicated abundances of biological molecules, created and ruled by genes.

He saw the stars' signs against the black sky and thought about the innumerable universes existing somewhere, behind a thin and unconceivable membrane. He marveled. But he didn't forget Rachel.

14

Winter came in force, bringing howling winds and towering snow drifts. Jack let snow cover the temple. He had supplies and organic farms inside and didn't have to go out for food. When he did go out, it was to let his thoughts run free and reach his hypnagogic state.

He plodded below the temple and saw young trees pushing through the snow. A few of them were almost ten feet high. Jack had made them grow as quickly as possible. With time, their genes would make them fill out and stabilize, but so far they were slender sprouts. Several had broken under snow or in storms.

That was all right. Their genotypes were self-repairing. Jack saw trees with open wounds, trees with scabs of black bark and trees with fading scars. His garden gave him a kind of peace.

This was not enough.

He still worked hard through all his waking hours. After lying in bed, trying to hold on to his dreams for as long as possible, he rose and had a light breakfast.

During the rest of the day, he dreamed on, and at night he went to bed and waited to drift off into sleep.

This may not sound like hard work but it actually was. Most of the time, his dreaming wasn't at all formless and random; on the contrary, it was purposeful and concentrated, all the way into his hypnagogic state. A kind of meditation, a single-minded and intentional effort.

His energy began to peter out.

Around midwinter, the storms ended and the sky was clear again. The sun dragged its way up over the horizon for a short hour in the middle of the day, but there was never any real daylight. The days had a surreal blue tinge; the sky was a pale blue, the long shadows on the bluish snow showed a darker hue, while the delicate birches and pines were sharply outlined in black against the vast expanses of bluish snow. Reindeer and elks, wolves and foxes, passed silently during the long nights. Their footprints wrote undecipherable messages in the snow. Crows called forlornly far away.

Jack didn't know how long he had stared into the blue twilight. He suddenly straightened. It was time for a break.

§

One or two days would be enough, he thought. He studied himself in a mirror of modified cornea with a backing of enamel. The sight wasn't uplifting: he had lost weight, his not very clean clothes hung loosely on his body, he was unshaven going on a full beard and his eyes seemed to have sunk into his face, almost disappearing, as if they were stuck in quicksand. The drowning eyes reminded him of his first face. Jack didn't want to meet his own gaze.

He showered for a long time, soaped himself over and over again, rinsed and soaped once more. Afterwards he cut his hair and shaved, this too slowly and pleasurably. While his clothes dried, he sat wrapped in a towel, vaguely thinking about the fact that he only owned one set of clothes. He had worn them all the way since he came back from Shylock.

He needed new clothes.

§

After looking for a while in the temple's many rooms and corridors, he found a clothes room. He jacked himself into a dream of clothes that would fit him perfectly and they immediately started growing, woven by a function originally found in wolf spiders. But the process would take a couple of days and he ascended stairs to put on his old clothes again.

He prepared food, this also carefully and pleasurably: he fried and boiled, instead of chewing a couple of sandwiches, standing up by the window. There was wine in a storage room next to the kitchen and he opened a glass bottle from the end of the previous country. He chose it simply because of the label.

Jack ate as slowly as he had cooked, relishing his jaws working, the feel of the fork against his lips. He moved the reindeer meat and vegetables to and fro in his mouth to feel every taste to the utmost. He rolled the wine on his tongue.

The wine was quite acceptable and made him nicely warm and heavy. He thought about opening another bottle but decided against it. Instead, he connected to the bionet and read the latest news.

While Jack was isolated in his temple life went on, in the colonies as well as on Earth. Jack read of catastrophes and miraculous escapes, of political squabbles and heroic interventions.

A couple in Mexico City, twenty-year-olds in their first bodies, had modified their bodies into images of the Aztec snake god Quetzalcoatl. All had seemed well until the woman became pregnant and it turned out that the modifications were somewhat more advanced than expected: the woman didn't carry a fetus, but about a thousand eggs. Indignant voices demanded that the eggs be aborted immediately; others tried to arrange support for the family that soon would be enormous; a few called out for a ban on all modifications not preceded by deep talks with experts, and preferably some kind of official permit.

The man and woman maintained that they were very happy. They planned to move to one of the old gaucho ranches in Argentina to bring up their family, their colony, there. Which shocked still more people: comments were full of computations about how long it would take a family, whose batches of children consisted of thousands, to fill not only the Earth but the entire known universe. Equally aggressive answers noted that this was the very reason why other planets were colonized.

An asteroid would collide with the moon in about a century and with a ninety percent certainty tear loose mile-wide pieces of rock. A few of these would, with equal certainty, collide with the Earth. A day in March, 2913, they would hit an area between Paris and Irkutsk. There was no reason to worry. A plan was set in motion. The asteroid would be blown to pieces by enormous modified fish bladders.

In Sydney, an opera singer had modified her own genome into a miniature copy of the famous old opera house. She has planned to tour with the living house, but it turned out that the house needed quite a lot more protein than the singer had calculated. She was now preparing for a support recital and appealed for people to attend.

An Icelandic scientist claimed that multis didn't exist. They were a collective hallucination, a kind of side effect from psychological traumas after the upheavals. But what about modified DNA? the scientist's opponents wrote aggressively. And the scientist answered in the same tone that the ability to manipulate your own genes was built into the genes themselves, and that it had only been a matter of time before humans would discover it.

The debate had ended with a huge public seminar in Reykjavik. Discussions had turned into screaming from both sides when a multi appeared on stage. The scientist who didn't believe in the creatures tried to run his hand through what he believed to be an illusion. He had lost parts of all four fingers and the stumps showed something that seemed to be a second-degree burn. The scientist himself held forth that what had happened was an example of the power of human imagination, just like the stigmatizations of old.

There was no news about war or famine.

Jack grew more and more tired as he read, watched and listened. He let weariness set in, he didn't think about anything in particular, strayed between more or less touching or shocking news. At his third drawn-out yawn, he got to his feet.

He went to bed, immediately fell asleep and slept without dreams.

§

He got out of bed as soon as he awoke the next morning. There was a supply room with skis and other winter supplies; Jack put on snow shoes and walked up above the rapids.

The light still was blue. The air was bitingly cold. Every breath was a sharp knife turning in his lungs.

Jack looked out at his world. The little forest defiantly popped its slight sprouts out of the snow. In the distance, snow fields billowed unbroken over the tundra.

Jack thought of nothing.

It was all just a break. A way of resting all functions that had grown exhausted during Jack's long and concentrated dreaming. He took another day off, cooked his food even more leisurely, drank one more bottle of wine, studied more news and gossip on the net.

His gaze stopped at a picture but he did not look at it. The picture suddenly had become meaningless. Something happened within Jack.

His break was over. His work called to him.

The glimpses of other universes grew more frequent and longer. After, at first, just seeing a face or a place flashing by in a fraction of a second, bringing home a confusing memory that slowly faded, he gradually became able to hold the glimpses for a few moments.

He soon realized that he was traveling in two different ways. The two ways corresponded to watching a holo or experiencing a virtual. In the first case, you saw a series of events from outside; in the second, you experienced it from somebody's point of view.

The first kind was psychological: only his soul or conscience traveled. He went into some other edition of himself, as a kind of passenger, just as he had watched his memories without really being there.

The second kind meant that even his body went to other universes.

The difference became obvious when he could stay and fight the rubber band, long enough to try to move in the other world. This might be something quite simple, like raising his arm or turning his head. Sometimes it worked, sometimes not.

Everything seemed just as clear and real in both cases. He saw, he heard, all his senses gave him vivid impressions. But sometimes he couldn't control his own body. At those times, he felt a kind of nausea. A strange dizziness, vertigo not related to height. He thought strange thoughts, fragments that he couldn't understand.

§

After a few days, he began to understand what was happening. When just his consciousness traveled, he went into other copies of himself. At the conscious level, his thoughts didn't seem to disturb, or be disturbed by, the thoughts of the Jack he had traveled into. At lower levels, something akin to the failed telepathy experiments happened: his own subconscious thoughts and unconscious processes mingled with the others in feedback and mirroring. Since he himself on other worlds had different thoughts, memories and processes, but still he was always *he*, none of the selves fell apart.

On the other hand, he did feel sick. And the experience of trying to lift his arm, and not being able to do so, was not pleasant.

The discomfort did not mean that Jack, even for a moment, thought about quitting. He fought down his nausea and swallowed, trying to chase away the disgust of a body that wouldn't obey. Sometimes trying to swallow and not succeeding brought him retching back to his own world. But over and over he tried again.

Returning into his own body, he was disoriented. Often he sat up, blinked and looked around in confusion. He needed a few seconds before he realized where he was. And who he was.

After a week or so, he found that it was easier to travel mentally. By now, he could manage ten or fifteen such trips a day, in spite of the nausea; he could withstand the power that tried to tug him back to his own world for more and more seconds. He also learned to relax and to trust his other edition's ability to keep his balance.

He wondered if the experience was as unpleasant for his counterpart as for himself.

$$\mathcal{S}$$

During a phase of a few days he doubted everything, questioned everything. Everything except his search. He doubted himself and the world. This might have been a tendency to depression or an effect of colliding with other copies of himself. Jack chose to believe the latter.

But he got used to it. He got used to it simply because he had decided to. And in time, traveling in the other way became easier.

At first, Jack didn't understand why he was able to travel in two ways. It might just be that the mental travels were simpler; after all, they were the first way he'd learned. But just in weeks, he was traveling almost as freely in his body.

Later, he found an explanation. There were innumerable worlds where Jack was dead, or where he had never been born. To travel to those worlds with just his psyche, he would have had to land in somebody else's consciousness. And that was impossible; it would have extinguished both selves as fast as the experiments with telepathy had.

Those were the worlds where he traveled with his body.

As he worked, he tried to express in words how traveling felt.

It always began with him entering the hypnagogic state. His mind was close to drifting off into dreams. He had no contact with his body, he didn't know who or what he was.

He was hovering in darkness over the waters.

And somewhere he saw a light. Sometimes several. The lights where white and bright or reddish and smoky. The fragments of consciousness left in him were drawn to one of the lights. He preferred the white and bright lights without knowing why.

Then he was in another world. That was when he started feeling the power, the rubber band trying to tug him back, a kind of weight not directed downwards or backwards but rather inwards, into himself. Towards some chakra or mental center of gravity where his own self was.

He held on for as long as he could. Then he gave in, let himself fall with the weight that was too heavy to carry. And blinked in confusion somewhere in his temple.

Certain memories lingered.

One time, he was suddenly filled with violent emotion. It was as if everything he had ever felt for Rachel, all his longing and regret, suddenly had gathered into one point, instead of being scattered over centuries. As if he had won Rachel again but immediately lost her.

He traveled mentally. The body he found himself in was on its knees. In front of it was a woman. Jack's eyes couldn't see more than her legs and midriff. Still, he knew this was Rachel. The woman's legs might have belonged to anybody, but he knew. Jack's mind reacted automatically and tried to lift his head. But the body was of another world and refused to obey. Jack heard it sobbing and reacted in panic. He let go and fell back into his own body.

The sight was hard to forget. The woman didn't move at all. She sat motionless before Jack without reacting to his sobbing.

For weeks, he wondered what had happened.

Another time, he was at an outdoor restaurant. The view was gorgeous. He was lucky; the body he was in was just taking in enormous snow-covered mountains and deep valleys. Jack recognized some detail and realized he was in the Himalayas.

Next to him was a woman. He could only see her from the corner of his eye but she might be Rachel.

Other glimpses were incomprehensible. A house that didn't look like any he'd ever seen: towers and pinnacles even on the towers and pinnacles, extra gables on the gables and oriels on the oriels. A labyrinth of windows and doors and corridors. Jack, or the body he was gate-crashing, stood in a window, looking out over the strange creation. Then he turned to a winding corridor.

A woman laughed somewhere and Jack knew who she was. He desperately tried to hold on but it was hopeless.

Another corridor, dark, with unpleasant cold luminous points in the ceiling. The air was even colder, damp and with a putrid smell. Two men were dragging him. He tried to resist but couldn't influence the body he was visiting. That body itself fought but was as helpless as Jack. The feeling of both trying to resist, and feeling somebody else doing this in the same body, made him sick. There was a door further down in the corridor, a rectangle of light; he didn't want to know; he let go.

Children laughing on a summer's day and Jack knew they were his. Everything was as it should be. He had everything he had ever wanted. A woman was sitting next to him but he only saw her from the corner of his eye.

He wanted to hold on but failed. Later, he tried to go back, but failed again.

Once he saw himself sitting at a plain dinner table. Rachel was opposite him. It was undoubtedly her and she looked exactly as he remembered her. She smiled. They talked about everyday things.

Jack wanted to return to this world, too. He never saw it again.

He didn't think he had ever visited the same world twice. Considering the number of universes, this was not surprising. Still, he wondered. Wouldn't a visit to another world open some kind of channel? A track through the multiverse, an association path, a road to travel?

He didn't know. But it would be some time before he saw the same world more than once.

One day, he managed to stay a little longer in a world. He was in a dense jungle. The air was unbearably hot. A big fly droned past his ear and landed on his arm. He saw that it wasn't a fly at all, rather some kind of big mosquito, and lifted his hand to squash it.

He *lifted his hand to squash it.*

His hand stopped in midair.

It might be a reflex, he thought.

The insect still sat on his forearm. He whacked at it, but it was gone as soon as he moved. But he actually decided himself. And he wasn't feeling sick.

A sound from a tree nearby made him turn. Two small lemur-like creatures, thin and ragged with enormous eyes, looked down at him. They might have reached up to his knees. They chattered excitedly to each other and pointed at him.

"Hi there," he said.

One of the lemurs did something to the other, maybe searching for flies or some other kind of grooming. The other just stared at Jack.

Jack had a definite feeling that he was looking at Rachel. This world's counterpart to Rachel: a small mammal on a planet with endless rain forests. With a partner who eagerly caressed and examined her body.

She still watched Jack with her large eyes. Jack waved to her as he felt the weight gather to pull him away.

Ha was joyful all that afternoon. It was quite silly, but he didn't harm anyone by being happy.

The thought of the little lemur and her partner warmed him.

15

Jack felt worn-out again. He hadn't seen the multi for some weeks. Since his son left the temple, he hadn't seen anybody at all.

He called for the multi. Reaching the creature was becoming more and more easy and it immediately appeared.

"You need others," he said to the multi, just to provoke a reaction. "Don't you? Sub-atomic particles interact, particles interact between universes, everything interacts. My conscience interacts with yours."

The multi showed agreement. Jack saw a picture of a single human being, static and unmoving. Another human appeared. The two influenced each other, made each other react, made each other change.

The new human disappeared. A moment later, the first one also vanished.

A few moments passed before Jack understood.

"Yes," he said. "A human being is the sum of her interactions with others. All alone, you will end up being nothing."

The multi bowed and gave Jack another lesson.

The multi let Jack see himself, sitting at his parents' breakfast table. Several years before the upheavals.

Jack's father seemed very tired. Hollow-eyed and dejected.

Jack was four or five, full of energy. He happened to knock his milk glass over.

His father yelled at him.

Jack was frightened and ran out from the room. He hid in a closet and cried.

New holo. Same scene, same breakfast, but Jack's father was in a good mood. Jack knocked the glass over. His father laughed and mopped up.

Afterwards, Jack sat in his father's lap, laughing.

The multi showed the two final moments at the same time: Jack crying in the closet, Jack laughing with his father.

Two arrows appeared above the pictures, pointing in different directions. And a question mark.

The smallest event could have enormous consequences. A man in old Berlin tried to hail a cab. He stepped right into the street and forced another car to slam on the brakes. The driver looked at his watch when he accelerated again. He was stressed. He didn't see what was happening before him and hit a young girl.

The girl was a top-level gymnast. She would never walk again.

A butterfly in Peking fell to the ground. A spider scampered over to the body. A little girl saw the spider and was scared. The girl ran away from her mother. A westerner spoke kindly to her, crouching, nodding and smiling. The girl went with the westerner. One year later, she was sold to a reclusive millionaire in Hong Kong. At first, the man abused her sexually, but in time, he fell in a kind of love with her. When he died, she was nineteen. He left her all his money. She went to the university, studied meteorology, and in time she moved to New York. Ten years later she discovered a method for controlling hurricanes.

A chaos of possibilities, missed and realized. Late trains. Unexpected meetings. Helpful people and others. A smile that made someone glad and got her to help somebody else; an angry word that made somebody hiss at his partner. A son falling sixty floors to the ground, a desperate father running past block after block to get to the site. A woman buying a scratch card, staring in confusion when she saw the enormous sum repeat for the third time.

Possibilities everywhere. Things that could happen.

If anything could happen, it would. In some universe. Somewhere.

Jack saw himself being born. A nurse noted the time of birth on a pad.

The picture split. In another universe, Jack was born one minute earlier.

"I see," Jack said presently. "Different moments in different universes. It might differ by one second in between two universes and by millennia between others.

The multi showed Jack's sister being born.

"I never had a sibling. But I might have had. And," Jack said, "you're repeating yourself. I already know this."

§

After a while, the multi managed to explain.

Of course, it was possible that a family had one, two or twenty children. And since all those variants were possible they happened in some universe.

The multi, however, was referring to something else. If a couple had two children, these might be born as twins; or with one year between them, or twenty. Both children might be girls or boys, or even hermaphrodites – even in this case, the possibilities were almost endless.

The children might be very alike or very different, depending on what genes they happened to carry in their universe. One child might grow up to be almost seven feet tall, inclined to corpulence and with a loud and grating voice, or turn out tiny and quiet. The other child might resemble its sibling or be quite different. The children might be of the same sex, or different sexes, and they might be born in different order.

"So if I'd had a sister, she might have been older or younger than me."

The multi agreed. It showed a picture of Jack and his possible sister.

The sister became a brother.

At first, the brother was very different from Jack. Then he changed; he gradually looked more and more like Jack; at last, the two were impossible to tell apart. They stood there, next to each other, exact copies.

The multi made them change places. Again. And again. They whirled for a few seconds. A question mark appeared above their heads.

"Right," Jack said. "If my sibling and I can be born at different times, before or after each other, and with different sets of genes ... and of course billions of experiences of different childhoods and adolescences ... then who is who?"

He watched the swirling multi and realized something.

"And that doesn't go just for siblings."

The multi showed Jack a picture that Jack immediately recognized: one of the most famous entertainers of the 20th century, the singer Michael Jackson. He had been a myth even when he was alive, and the myth had lived on after his death. Jackson had been one of the first humans to re-make his body and his strange, ever-changing face had been well known long before the upheavals.

Jack nodded.

In Jack's world, Jackson had been born in the year 1958. Jack now saw him born in 1960, 1961, 1963, later and later.

Jack himself had been born in 2032. They met, not in one single year, but in a very large zone; Jack and Michael Jackson might have been born in the same moment, at least from 1940 and up to 2050.

A cloud swirled, slowly changing from Jack's face to Jackson's.

"Who is who? Where is the boundary between me and him?"

A new cloud. Ten, hundred, innumerable faces. All with their traces backwards and forwards, their possible births during thousands of years. Whirling. And the question mark.

The borders were blurred. If Jack had been born ten years earlier, would he have been Jack? The Jack born ten years later in another universe, was he Jack?

The thought was dizzying. Every human flowed. In their own universe they were themselves, sharp and defined. But when you studied a hundred or a thousand universes nearby they soon became indistinct. And after many billions of universes every human was such a blurred cloud of possibilities that she started blending into others. Age, looks, sex, childhood, everything blurred together and became difficult to tell apart from other humans nearby.

At last, only the immense cloud existed.

The cloud showed all possibilities, everything that was possible given the laws of nature, for all possible human beings. All humans were aspects of the thinkable.

"At last," Jack said slowly, "all humans are the same ... The variants of me and Michael Jackson or anybody else are so innumerable and diverse that we turn into each other. At last, everybody is an aspect of everybody else ..."

Just different possibilities. More or less different expressions of DNA. There must be individuals somewhere who were just in the middle, half Jack, half Rachel – half anybody, half anybody else. Still, they were distinct personalities. You might choose anyone, and around that person would be quadrillions of versions, gradually changing, but still no doubt her or him; you might choose another and see the same thing happening. It was like the gradual change from young to old. You might see a fifteen-year-old, a forty-year-old and an eighty-year-old version of the same human and easily tell them apart. But what about the thirty-year-old person and herself ten minutes later? A tenth of a second later?

Jack was stupefied. Somewhere in the enormous cloud of human possibilities was the Rachel he searched: one single human being, in one single universe, one single time. Or rather, millions of copies in millions of universes – which, in the endless multiverse, amounted to the same.

"I'm beginning to see why I haven't found her yet," he murmured.

He looked at the tall swirling shape that was the multi and realized something. He was on the verge of asking the question when the multi went on.

Jack saw a double helix. The helix diffused into the cloud of possibilities, it became the cloud. The cloud thinned in places and thickened in others.

"What?"

Jack saw a holo of his own home and the rapids, seen from above.

The holo showed a starry night with bluish snow and moonlight. The white enamel of the temple shimmered.

The holo zoomed outwards and up. The temple dwindled and soon disappeared. Jack recognized the landscape that had been northern Sweden. Then Europe.

He saw the planet contract below him. The solar system.

Constellations shrunk, changed shapes, disappeared into a cloud of dim light. The galaxy receded at dizzying speed.

More galaxies receded and disappeared.

The picture split and split again. It showed the multiverse.

The picture of the DNA helix was superimposed over the fleeing galaxies. Over and over again. But every time, the spiral changed. It twisted, moved, grew and shrunk.

The number of possible combinations of DNA, and the number of lives possible to live by beings created from DNA, wasn't infinite. Not mathematically. But it was so enormously vast that even the multi couldn't really describe it.

Everything that was possible in the multiverse had to happen. The enormous cloud showed possibilities. And the possibilities had to be realized.

Jack didn't know why the multi had showed him all this. Maybe it had been some kind of preparation.

The vision had made him forget the question he wanted to pose. But in his subconscious, the question remained: sometimes he dreamed of the tall multi, but then Rachel filled his dreams again and he forgot.

A few weeks later, at the end of January, when the sun had the strength to climb higher in the sky and the blue light turned an almost unbearably white glare over the snow, he had seen thousands more possibilities in other universes. He had seen Rachel and himself as chimpanzees, as eagles, and as some kind of six-legged creatures that had no name in Jack's universe. He had seen Rachel alone as a two-year-old, in her thirties, in her nineties; in inconceivably modified bodies; healthy, sick, dying, newly born.

Billions of worlds. But he didn't give in. He wouldn't give in.

§

Spring quietly sneaked up on him as he worked.

Now and then, he had his breaks. He didn't want to lose contact with reality. He remembered pictures of people that had left society, hermits who had withdrawn from the world: white-bearded, with lank hair and long sharp nails. Mumbling incomprehensibly to themselves.

He took his breaks, if more and more reluctantly, when he felt himself moving in that direction. He rested for a few days. He went for walks, watched news on the bionet.

During a break in April, the multiverse tugged at him, and he was just about to leave the net when he heard a word that made him react. He sat down again.

Shylock.

The colony had come to an end.

He went to text and quickly scanned.

Everybody was dead.

The planet, or rather its biology, had run amok. The barren lands had gradually turned lush. At some time, the change had reached a critical point and turned exponential. Nobody had been prepared when mutated spores spread through the air, filling the colonists' lungs with quickly growing ferns.

This was my fault, Jack thought. I should have fought for my idea. Things may have turned out differently.

There were other possibilities. Somewhere else in the multiverse, I fought and had my way. The colony might have survived.

But not in this world. All the colonists were dead. The last radio message had hardly been intelligible: the man sending it became more and more unintelligible, gasped out his last words, suffocated in front of the microphone as the ferns exploded in his lungs.

This had happened thirty-two years ago.

It must have happened just months since Liya sent her message to Jack.

And now, she was back on Earth again.

The genomes of the dead were in vaults on Earth, as well as their memories. Now, bodies would quickly be grown. In just a few months, the colonists would have their memories and selves back.

They could choose between staying on Earth or going to some other colony planet.

All they had lost was their time on Shylock. Those memories were gone. There might be some vault on the planet where the colonists had uploaded their new memories, but it was hardly probable that someone would take the trouble of going thirty-two light-years round trip again.

The colonists would awake believing that their education had recently been completed and that they were landing on Shylock.

Jack wondered what Liya would feel. But this was just a fleeting thought. Before he was on his feet, his dreams were moving into the multiverse again.

Somewhere was Rachel. The Rachel he sought.

Liya was forgotten again, a pale shadow from the past. Jack let his obsession wash over him like a wave, fill him, become him. This felt like modifying his genes, and maybe that was exactly what he was doing; maybe the feeling of adrenalin or endorphins pumping into his system meant that he actually was changing. He hoped so.

He dreamed of eyes smiling at him seven centuries earlier, let them wash over him, let himself drown in them.

16

Of course, he thought, he should travel physically. What would it gain him to enter some other Jack's body? To feel sick from the contact of a mind that was almost his own, almost but not quite? And having no way of controlling a body that wasn't quite his own?

Also, he had realized that if he went on traveling mentally, sooner or later he would find himself in a sex act. This act might involve any woman or man. It might involve Rachel. That thought was unbearable. He didn't want to experience somebody that was almost himself in the most intimate of moments, captured in a body that he couldn't control, desperately longing for the woman who lustfully gave herself to somebody almost but not quite himself.

He traveled physically.

The visit to the jungle planet with the lemurs had been a kind of breakthrough. The process was like learning a new language, or maybe learning to ride a bicycle. One day, something happened and the balance was there. He knew that he would fall, lose contact with the world he was visiting, many more times. But he became better and he kept working.

He came to a world where he saw Rachel here, in his own temple, far off in the north, but a world where the tundra was replaced with lush jungles as far as he could see. She sat on the top white terrace with a baby in her arms. Strange feelings raged through Jack as he hurried up to her.

She raised her head to look at him. She was incredulous.

"But you're dead," she said. Her eyes brimmed with tears and the unfathomable weight dragged Jack back to his own world.

Jack breathed heavily. So close. He had been just a couple of feet from her.

Was the child his? Had he recently died in that world?

Why had he been thrown back here?

But, he realized, this proved that it could work. He tried to think positive thoughts. It was possible to travel, it was possible to find Rachel. It was even possible to find a Rachel that wanted him.

The next time, he was in a big house close to a beach. He couldn't say where. The landscape didn't look like the tropics, or like his own northern world. The sea was greenish and the ground rose dramatically to high mountains.

The house was bright with sunlight and beautiful. Room after room with white walls, sparsely furnished. A few paintings here and there showed people with young and beautiful bodies.

Outside the paintings, Jack saw no one at all.

He waited.

It was unusually easy to hold on. Jack stayed for what felt like an hour. He walked through the house and familiarized himself with it: a kitchen, a big dining room and an equally big parlor, on the bottom floor. Two more floors with bedrooms and rooms whose function Jack couldn't guess.

From one of the bedrooms on the top floor, he saw the first human being. It was a man, dressed in some kind of overalls. He worked hard, digging in the ground. He straightened to quickly wipe sweat from his forehead, looked around and immediately bent over his shovel again. He worked hard, pushing on, seeming almost manic.

Jack wondered why the man didn't use biologic aids.

At last, she came. Jack was in the rooms facing the sea and didn't see her approaching the house. He heard her step when she came in and immediately went that way.

Rachel. His Rachel. Standing by a cupboard in the kitchen.

She was dressed in white, black hair reaching down to her waist. Her face showed no surprise.

"Are you home?" she said. "I thought you were on that colony planet."

"Shylock?" he said, taken aback. "But that was in another –"

Rachel shrugged. "Yeah, I guess that was it. But –," she suddenly smiled and something happened inside Jack – "here you are now."

"Yes. How have you been?" He spoke empty phrases while trying to think. Was he really thirty-two light-years away? Was it possible to exist in two copies in the same universe? If they were sufficiently far apart?

Or maybe, he realized, the version of him gone to Shylock had died. Maybe with lungs full of ferns.

"Fine," she said. "I'm always fine. You were the one who had problems."

"Well, I'm back now."

She went on putting groceries in the cupboard. Then she suddenly stopped and turned to him. "So are you feeling better now?"

Meaning that something had bothered him. Made him go to Shylock. He tried to read her face.

"If we can be together," he chanced.

"I've never minded. You were the one who ..."

Who what? he wondered.

"Maybe I've realized what's important," he tried his way.

She took a couple of steps towards him. Rachel, his dream. So close. He could see true joy in those eyes.

"Really?"

"Really."

One more step. She was almost in his arms when she stopped. Bit her lip. Looked up at him again.

"So ... no more protests about the slaves?"

"Slaves?" he said.

And the weight tore him away.

It made sense, he thought later. The man in the overalls. Heavy work, no biological aids. Quick and furtive glances while he rested.

A world with slave labor. And Rachel seemed to have accepted it. But not Jack.

Jack thought about this for days. Would it have been worth it to stay in that world?

No, he decided. The Rachel in that world might look exactly as the Rachel he remembered, she might look at him with those eyes that made his entire being melt, her body might drive him mad, she could be infinitely loving and caring to him. Still, she wouldn't be the same Rachel. She wouldn't be the woman he loved.

Maybe that was what had thrown him back. An unexpected emotional reaction. In the world before that one, Rachel had said that he was dead, and he had immediately found himself in his own world again. In this world, he had realized there were slaves. None of the concepts appealed to him.

When he found the perfect world, nothing would drag him home. All feelings would make him stay. He would be Jack and Rachel would be Rachel. Together for as long as their genomes could create new bodies.

They would store millennia of happiness in memory banks.

§

After the trip to the slave world, Jack needed couple of days off before he could travel again. Something had disturbed him; realizing that Rachel was alive and happy in a slave world gnawed at him.

Naturally, he admonished himself: You are like that, too, in some other universe. Everything that can happen must happen and there are worlds where Rachel left you to go to another world, free of slavery.

He repeated this to himself, over and over. Everything that can happen must happen. Don't be discouraged. Better worlds exist, good worlds, and you will reach them. You will reach them.

A new summer swept in with numbing beauty. The birches below the temple burst into transparent light green leaf. The darker hues of spruces and pines completed the color range. The air heated and evenings became long and sunlit. Migrating birds came, hares changed color, reindeer passed on their way from the coast; and Jack worked.

He came to a world of what had been called devil worship.

Most other people in Jack's home world wouldn't even have understood what was happening. The Christianity still left seven centuries after the upheavals sometimes mentioned Hell, described as a nothing, a separation from God and eternal bliss; but the devil himself had been cleansed from the mythology.

But Jack was old. He could remember the cults that had grown more and more strong as the upheavals closed in. Burning churches, vandalized graveyards, rumors of human sacrifice, murder and torture – everything that had appeared during the second half of the 20th century gained ground, as the end of the world no longer was a ghost at the horizon but became gradually more real. During the last years, when the wars had already begun, Jack had seen Satanists in their brown cowls walk into woods or up mountains to perform their rites: once the hooded people dragged with them a young girl, helplessly screaming and wriggling to get free; nobody helped her and when the group had disappeared into the trees, her screams slowly faded.

Jack remembered.

He had worked hard, without progress, for three days. He was surprised when he was suddenly thrown into another world.

People in brown cowls. In a circle.

The night was dark. No moon, but stars like pinpricks. The people in the cowls chanted. In the middle of the circle, a naked girl writhed on a stone.

Jack had no time to see more. The weight threw him back to his temple.

He breathed heavily.

Rachel must have been there. Rachel must have been one of the people in the cowls.

The girl on the stone. A sacrifice. Or, he tried to calm himself, some kind of sexual rite. Nothing proved that the girl would be sacrificed. He hadn't seen anything indicating that she was in trouble. Nothing at all.

He tried to calm himself but failed. Deep within, he knew. And Rachel had been there.

This isn't good, Jack thought. Not good at all.

He sat in the summer sun. The sky was blue, infinitely high, and small white clouds lazily drifted at the southwest horizon. His world was beautiful.

He tried to think clearly.

He might be attracted to such worlds by chance. Two times was a weak statistical basis. Worrying was silly.

Still, he worried.

The multi had talked about DNA, about how slight or important similarities between worlds were expressed in genomes and how it would be easier for Jack to travel to worlds where these expressions were quite like his own. But this must apply to some aspect or dimension of the genome that Jack didn't understand. He remembered the jungle planet and the small lemurs. Their genes couldn't be very like his own and Rachel's.

Or, he realized, they might be. They could hold the very potential that would develop to himself and Rachel two million years later. Or maybe the lemurs, on their planet, were the form of humanoids that were closest to him and her.

He wished he had been in that world. Without consciousness, happy with his female.

Yes, he thought, it might be about potential. Like all other creatures in the multiverse, he had almost infinite potential. Rachel, too. Her potential he could see realized, but not his own: when he traveled physically there was no living Jack in the worlds he visited, and when he traveled mentally he probably couldn't make contact with psyches that were too alien to him, psyches that might take slavery or human sacrifice for granted.

But such versions of him had to exist. And he had to accept that there were innumerable editions of Rachel that he wouldn't like at all. He remembered the skeleton-like woman in Rio and shuddered.

Do not give up, he told himself. I will not give up. She is somewhere, and I will find her.

He tried to think of ways to find worlds that he liked, worlds where he could imagine living. It had to be possible to guide his travels. If not, he thought over and over again – if not, and if I find myself in the very worlds I'm dreaming of, but get torn away from it – how could I find my way back?

§

He tried concentration and meditation, guided dreams, ganja and other drugs that he ordered from Morocco and California. He ate mushrooms and licked toads. He experienced hundreds of worlds.

Day after day, his shadow went around him on the wide enamel terrace. He stood there in the Kayotsarga posture, alone in the sunshine.

Things weren't sharply defined and delimited any more.

He seemed to touch the multiverse. Millions of other Jacks stood in the same yoga posture. The shadows crawling around them mixed together and created diffraction patterns, bands of light and shadow, unreadable messages from other worlds.

§

One day he glimpsed, just for a few seconds, a world where the body was holy. A world where man was his own temple. Everything pertaining to the body was worshipped; secretions and waste were as public and natural as meals. Jack was astounded and let himself be torn away. Later, he was ashamed for his visceral reaction, much stronger than in the slavery world.

In another world, reason was divine. Feelings were seen as obsolete and Rachel, in a handy pantsuit, her hair cropped and her body slim, listened thoughtfully while Jack talked.

He knew he didn't want to stay here. But one day he would find the world he wanted, and he took the opportunity to rehearse what he would say.

"And by now I have been searching for you for almost a year. In world after world. I want to find a world where we can be happy together."

"Happiness," Rachel said, "cannot be static. Happiness is a short and momentary anomaly in our normal state. Being happy all the time would make happiness meaningless."

He gestured. "You know what I mean."

Rachel started to speak but he let himself go home again.

He thought: I travel by dreaming. I can concentrate at first, but finally, I will dream. Consciousness has to be disconnected.

I have never consciously thought about Rachel's age or looks. I know whom I'm dreaming of, and I go to worlds where she is.

That is what I must work on. I must teach my subconscious to find the right kind of Rachel, impress this on the parts of my psyche that I don't know myself. The parts that make it possible for me to travel.

He came closer. Closer and closer, snapshot by snapshot.

But he never really made it all the way. Something was always wrong.

I am possessed, he thought as the leaves of the birches grew yellow again. I should abandon this. Get rid of my memories, not just hide them in some vault but burn them. Burn them and spread the ashes. Create a new existence with somebody who is as different from Rachel as possible.

That would never happen. He knew he'd tried before. He must have stood ready to destroy his memories, brandishing a flame-thrower or something similar; but at the last moment, he had changed his mind. It was his entire life, he'd told himself, memories from seven centuries. How could he destroy them? And also, the interference would always make his dreams come back.

He had to find her. Didn't his thoughts about finding someone else prove that he was stuck in her world? Wasn't the thought of somebody different a symptom of this?

All he wanted was to find her. There was nothing else in his universe.

More and more worlds. Always something wrong. He could stay longer by now; he had spoken for quite a while with many editions of Rachel, stayed in some worlds, even learned to return to them. This might work for an evening, or three times, or a week.

Then, he found something that as wrong. Her smile wasn't as dazzling as his memories; her skin not as soft.

Her views might bother him. She didn't have to advocate slavery, but she might feel that the world should be governed in another way. That Jack's riches should give him more power. That somebody, maybe herself, should have the right to decide about things like biological modifications.

"A snake god," one of her said, for that had happened in her world, too, "a snake god, how could somebody modify themselves to that? A thousand eggs? That's madness. I'd never allow something like that." And before even thinking about her words, Jack was back in his temple.

The time when Jack stayed a whole week, what made him leave was one silly little detail. In that world, Rachel was, if possible, more beautiful than he remembered her. She was gentle and graceful, and for days, he thought that he'd finally found the one he was looking for.

Just one little detail bothered him.

Her laughter was a tiny bit cackling.

She was happy to have him back, she had a big and warm heart and often laughed. At first, Jack smiled a little at the sound. Then he began waiting for it. He tried to smile again but it was hard. The sound irritated him.

She didn't stop laughing. His irritation grew.

On the seventh night, he left. He watched her face, sleeping peacefully beside him, and wished her luck. She didn't know from whence he'd come; since he didn't exist in worlds where he could travel physically, he always invented stories about how he had created a new body or returned from a colony. Rachel would understand that he had left her. Maybe she would try to find him, but he wouldn't be in her world.

The thought made him sad.

But he couldn't stand her cackling.

For maybe a day, he had some regrets. Couldn't he have accepted this silly detail? Learned to live with it? No, he knew himself too well. And thinking about this, he suddenly realized that everything that was happening also was true in reverse: there had to be a Rachel – millions – searching for him in the same way he was trying to find her.

Millions of Rachels, finding small defects in millions of Jacks, maybe something in their facial expressions, their choice of words, or their way of getting to their feet. It could be anything. His first reaction was to protest – he was who he was, right? – but then he thought: so was the cackling girl I left. I was unfair.

He didn't change his mind. He knew exactly what he wanted.

§

Yes, he thought, as the first snows came; he was possessed.

He gave himself time until the winter solstice. When the world was at its darkest he would make up his mind: either he would have found the one right Rachel, or be so close that going on was worthwhile. If not, he would give up, create a lemur's body and go to live in the strips of jungle left in Africa.

No. Not like that. First of all, of course it wouldn't work, and then he also knew that he wouldn't even try.

But he had to find something. Some way of getting out of this.

All the copies of Rachel had in common that they recognized him, and knew him. He never had to tell them who he was, just listen to their stories of how he'd died or disappeared or emigrated to Rigel. Then he invented some neat explanation. And after that, it was like meeting after a long trip. They knew each other inside and outside and it was almost like coming home.

But no more than almost. There was always some nagging detail. At last, Jack started to believe that he was looking for that detail. That something in him didn't want things to be perfect.

The night before midwinter, he made his last try. He avoided all kinds of drugs and instead emptied his brain by physical exhaustion; he skied in the soft snow all day, seven hours in one stretch, without eating or drinking anything. The stars glittered in the black sky when he left his skis at one of the portals. He went in, took a long and hot shower and had a light meal. Then he dreamed.

He didn't get anywhere. He saw many worlds, he allowed himself to play with the notion of staying, but somehow, it was too late. Rachel after Rachel passed in his dreams, one more beautiful than the other, more alluring than the third. Jack was allured, but right at the outset he knew that something would go wrong.

He gave up and got himself blind drunk.

This was the first time since Shylock. He wasn't quite that far gone, and he didn't have to throw up. Still, he could feel it the next day. He was extremely dehydrated and drank gallons of water. His stomach loudly protested and his head swam and ached. He thought: Never again. Never ever again.

It was time to find a new way.

Jack lay in bed, thinking, that whole day. Apart from his head and stomach, all his muscles tortured him after skiing the day before. He lay as still as he could.

Maybe a thousand universes, he thought. Maybe more. At least, not less. I have visited at least a thousand universes and stayed for a day or more in maybe fifty of them. I have spoken to hundreds of Rachels, old and young, happy and sad, blonde and dark, friendly and hostile. None of them is good enough for me.

There is only one Rachel. And she can't be here. She only exists in one place and in one time.

17

"If I can travel between universes," Jack said to the billowing shape in front of him, "and if different times, different snapshots or moments, just are special cases of different universes ... in that case, I should be able to travel in time, too?"

Yes, the multi's pictures told him. That was possible.

In principle, it wasn't even harder to travel so to speak vertically, in time, than horizontally, in space.

Jack methodically started studying to go backwards in time.

By and by, he would be able to find his way back to his night with Rachel. The only snapshot among billions of universes that he cared about.

Once again, the multi taught him. Jack saw pictures of how multis lived. He was amazed.

Humans had a "now" that lasted from less than a tenth of a second and up to about seven seconds. Measuring this was difficult, as the experience of time changed as soon as you thought about it. In certain situations, for example if many things happened in quick succession, a long now was harder to perceive: in a calm and meditative condition, a longer now could feel natural.

Close to the now were events, experiences, thoughts and feelings that were "almost now." The quickest forms of short-term memory made it possible to retrieve a few words that you'd missed as they were said: somehow, it was possible to re-live the moment.

People could also guess what would happen during the next moments. The vase will fall. You will make it. Don't go into the street. Don't put that in your mouth!

Foresight and hindsight made the now even more blurred. Like the multis, the now had no defined limits.

Jack learned that the now for a multi could last over thousands of years.

When a multi showed itself to people on Earth it wasn't really "one multi." It was millions of editions of the being, from as many universes. A few of them were a hundredth of an inch to the left. Others to the right. Some an inch closer, others further away.

This was a normal distribution: most in the middle, a few at the edges. Which was how the multis got their blurred appearance.

This was also the reason why it hurt or could even be dangerous to touch multis, that burning or pricking feeling. Before you touched what seemed to be the kernel of the creature, you had already grazed thousands of other editions, interfering with each other in a cloud of quantum possibilities, suddenly turning real inside your skin.

And of course, this was also the reason why the multi's picture messages were blurred. They came from millions of editions of the same being. Editions that would choose slightly different pictures, or combine the pictures in slightly different ways.

Jack realized that "his" multi was an entire host, a multitude, of creatures. For the second time, an idea glimmered in him.

He wondered what the multi wanted of him.

Multis had selves consisting of millions and a now reaching past thousands of years. Multis saw the world in quite a different way from humans.

Multis could watch a zone of billions of universes and snapshot as a whole. From the perspective of the eternal, the multi communicated with some effort; Jack recognized the phrase but couldn't place it.

Being a human, the multi said, you cannot see the world in this way. Each and every one of your editions helplessly travels through one single track of snapshots. Like a planet travels around its sun: it is possible to calculate where the planet, and you, will be in ten or a hundred years.

For us, the multi said, with our way of seeing the world, it is as if you humans were falling helplessly through time. Different versions of a planet have different trajectories in different universes. The versions of you travel quite as predictably through other trajectories, other series of snapshots.

"Meaning there is no free will?" Jack said.

The multi didn't answer. It went on.

Every choice Jack made – if he chose to search for Rachel or not; if he chose to stand up or remain sitting – moved him to different universes. Important choices, like trying to find Rachel, had obvious consequences. Smaller choices, like standing up, could also have drastic consequences, for example hitting his head; in other cases, small choices may not have noticeable consequences.

But every choice meant moving to another snapshot. Another universe.

The multi showed Jack the concept of a Planck time: the shortest meaningful time interval in all known universes, 10^{-43} seconds.

Jack had a hard time understanding.

Just think of something very short, the multi told him. Imagine a millionth of the wing stroke of a fly. Imagine a millionth of that time. Go on a number of times.

"I see," Jack said presently.

Doing nothing at all also meant moving between universes: between the snapshots in the "same" universe – like Jack sitting alone in his dining room, not moving, and Planck times rushing by at a rate of 18,550,948,324,478,400,000,000,000,000,000,000,000,000,000 a second. Sitting immovable, thinking of nothing at all, calmly breathing, he was transported between snapshots as surely, if not as dramatically, as anyone hunting six-legged buffalo in the North American prairies.

But not even multis knew where free will entered into this. Sometimes, they might see most of Jack's editions acting in a certain way. Did this mean free will? If eighty percent of Jack acted in a certain way, was this a better sign that "Jack," in all his existences, wanted this more strongly than if only fifty-five percent of him acted that way?

The multi seemed to think that free will didn't exist.

"But I can choose," Jack said eagerly. "I can choose to look for Rachel in time!

The multi answered: So you can.

"Will I succeed?"

Many of you must succeed. The question is if this edition of you will be one of them.

Once again, Jack experienced the burning feeling on his tongue when the multi gave him new DNA. And then he dreamed.

He began by traveling mentally.

Once again, it was high summer, and Jack stood, dressed in white, on the white enamel surface. He had abandoned yoga and now moved slowly in a measured, tranquil and thousands of years old Chinese form of gymnastics. The sun made him sweat and cast indistinct shadows towards the rectilinear portals in the copy of Hatshepsut's temple, light and dark bands, diffraction patterns flowing in and out of each other.

To multis, he thought as he neared the multiverse, "now" is both when this gymnastics is created and when I perform it. To them, I am one of billions, just in this world, moving in almost the exact same way, almost simultaneously.

But to me, I am just me.

He used an antique watch, a relic from a time long before the upheavals, with a mechanism that he had to wind up. He focused on the watch. Let himself be drawn into the rhythmic ticking. He devoted all his concentration to the second hand. Day after day he imagined it moving heavier, slower, until it would at last stop.

One day he succeeded.

The second hand of the watch wasn't the only thing that stopped. All of nature became silent and motionless. Not before the whispers of his little forest ended did he understand what a natural part of his life that sound had become.

A big bird, maybe a wader but it was hard to tell at this distance, hovered frozen above the temple. There was a noise, reminiscent of the forest's whispers but closer, more intimate. Jack realized he was hearing the blood in his veins.

Outside of him, all was frozen, immovable, until he gave in to the weight and let himself be yanked back. The second hand jumped twenty-eight seconds forward.

He worked on, dreamed in concentration during days and without control at night. His nightly dreams were fluid, elusive, undecided. It was hard to tell when he dreamed and when he was awake.

He lazily floated in a sea: green swell under him, piercing sun above. Not before he noticed that the sea wasn't water but genes did he realize that he was dreaming.

Stopping time became simple. He started working backwards: at first, the second hand crawled forward at a snail's pace; then it stopped; and began moving backwards, first slowly, reluctantly, then faster and faster, followed by the minute hand and the hour hand.

In a few days, he didn't need the watch anymore.

One day or night he dreamed of Shylock. The planet was empty and deserted. Biology had run amok and bizarre creations slithered along beaches, covered mountains, filled the seas. Everything fed on everything else. Jack didn't know if this was a nightmare or reality.

And then, one morning, he was back preparing for the journey to the colony planet. He spoke to Liya, a girl whose large eyes fascinated him. They joked about the new bodies they would have at arrival and whether they would be able to recognize each other.

Jack suddenly felt queasy. He bent over and Liya gave him a worried look.

"What's the matter?"

"Oh, nothing," Jack heard himself say. He tried to say something else but couldn't; he recognized the queasiness and knew that he was traveling in time. "Nothing at all."

Liya smiled at him. The power tore at him and he gave in.

Further back. The training before Shylock. The desperation before that. Jack visited time periods whose memories he hadn't opened since he came home. He relived his earlier efforts to break free. These weren't limited to living on colony planets: he had experimented with other women, with men, with groups; with strange forms of sex; with alcohol and many kinds of drugs. He had tried ruining himself until his heart gave in and he had changed bodies, over and over again, doggedly determined that the chemicals would make him free.

Nothing had worked.

He went back, further and further back. Sometimes, he doubted that he was on the right track. Finding his way back in time was like exploring the root system of an enormous tree, or like finding his way through a garden of forking paths; at every junction, he might choose the wrong way.

He trusted his queasiness. This became worse and worse the further back he went. For every decade or century, his consciousness became less and less like the person he was now. He fought the nausea and gradually overcame it.

Sometimes, his nausea suddenly grew much worse and he realized that he had gone to both another time and another world. He quickly retraced his steps.

The paths led him back and at last he arrived.

§

Yet again, he relived the most important night of his life. He sat at the table and felt his head turn, his eyes throw glances, over and over again. Towards Rachel. He talked to the other girl, Anna; this time, he could see how she watched him in the same way he watched Rachel, how she took every opportunity to move closer and closer to him. He heard his younger self deny his interest in Rachel, relived his uninterested responses to Anna's attempts to discuss astrology, accepted wine when she offered it.

The queasiness was there all along, as a shadow across his mind. It got worse when Rachel disappeared with Max.

They're just children, he thought. Children in their original bodies.

The thought made him sad.

Young Jack rose and went towards the cottage where he lived. Outside the yard, the forest was dark. His steps were slow and heavy. Joyless.

And then the whisper.

"Jack!"

Joy beyond words.

Somehow, this was stronger than reliving the memories. When he replayed his memories, he had been aware that that was what he was doing. This time, for long stretches, he was really *there*. He felt the weight of her breast, the smoothness of her thigh, the muscles playing under her skin. He relived every caress and every kiss yet again, intense enough to make him completely forget the nausea; yet again, he was totally, flash-lit, aware of every down of her body, every detail of her face, every time her eyes smiled at him. He let himself be trapped by her eyes to immediately drown in her mouth. They played silly games, she teasingly held him down, he tried to get free.

Storms were followed by calm. Soon, soft whispers were suc-

ceeded by gasps when fingers or lips brushed somewhere. Calm
caresses built to a new storm.

Jack saw and felt everything happen. Yes, he thought, this was
stronger. He was there. This was no memory: he was there. He really
was there. It was happening.

He watched his younger self. He saw himself filled by the happiness that he now remembered so well, the happiness that had made
him fell like somebody else; and now, seven hundred years later, he
wondered if the younger Jack somehow had felt his older self visit
him. Maybe that was what had made the night so special. Maybe his
younger self hadn't just been full of his own experiences but also
of those of the older Jack, the memories and expectations that his
present self brought.

This was impossible, he tried to soberly tell himself as the last
storm rose to its climax. That would be a paradox, and such paradoxes didn't exist in the multiverse: the world he visited right now,
exactly because he was here, wasn't the world he remembered. But
of course, there was the interference ...

$$\S$$

He cursed himself. Why was he thinking of that? There was no point
in wasting the last minutes by meaningless speculation. Just a little
while now, and Rachel would be gone.

His thoughts wouldn't leave him alone. Irritation took the upper
hand. He let himself fall back to his own time, his own now, before
the night even ended.

Later, he tried to rationalize. He sat in the middle of the top terrace, drinking a glass of water. The afternoon sun would soon hide
behind the temple and he could see shadows furtively emerging.
The water from the river was ice-cold and lovely.

It would soon have been over, he told himself. After what he'd
seen, only sadness remained. Well, almost; the morning had been
beautiful, that was true. He had worked in the scorching sun, reliving his memories, not at all tired.

But then, the supervisor had found him. "You're not needed anymore." Jack had packed his belongings, nobody but Anna had said goodbye, and he had walked south.

He had even turned back, he remembered. After walking for more than an hour. But he hadn't been able to contact Rachel. Somebody had told her father what had happened, possibly a jealous Max, and Jack could only hurt her by appearing at her home again.

Reliving that was useless. Those memories weren't better than the gaunt and bulimic Rachel in Rio.

That must be it, he tried to tell himself. He had let himself fall back here to avoid the sad memories.

But still.

§

But still. Hadn't he been brooding all night? Even during the first storms, while they were helpless in each other's arms? Hadn't he been analyzing instead of experiencing – hadn't he actually been thinking about how strong his experiences had been, instead of letting himself get caught up in them?

Jack rose. He drained the glass and turned to the sinking sun.

He didn't want that to be the case. When he finally had traveled back, journeyed seven centuries back to Rachel, it just couldn't be that he'd been analyzing. No way.

But still, he felt that that had happened.

Furthermore, something else was bothering him.

If nothing had been bothering him, he realized, he wouldn't even have brooded in this way. The very suspicion that something was wrong meant that ... something was wrong.

He knew interference was getting to him.

He angrily threw the glass from him. It smashed to pieces on the lowest terrace. Cleaning animals, modified from armadillos and anteaters, immediately scurried over the white surface, sucking the splinters into their armored trunks and disappearing into their lairs again. Jack remained standing where he was.

He was devastated.

He had searched for more than a year. Today, he should have been closer than ever. But it didn't feel that way. Something inside him had rebelled, analyzing instead of living.

It's this dreaming, he thought angrily, just what makes it possible for me to travel: that quality always makes me be in some other place, some other time, than where my body is.

No, he immediately protested, that's not right. The traveling happens when I actually forget time and space.

Still, he had been analyzing, as if he'd watched a boring holo and started dreaming.

To be analytic when he relived the most important night in his life was unacceptable. Thinking afterwards would have been all right, to remember what happened, to think of possibilities that were real in other worlds.

But to devote yourself to that while the most important event in your life happened – that was out of the question.

He called for the multi again. The multi, shimmering, listened.

The multi said, I told you there was a cost.

Jack didn't understand

Your travels. Other worlds, other times. I told you it might cost you.

"You knew this would happen?"

The multi showed Jack a picture of a shrug.

It was possible, it said. And since it was a possibility, it had to become real in some world or worlds. You took a risk.

Jack said, "I'm not going to give up."

His own words surprised him. But he knew they were true.

"I'm not going to give up," he said again. "I'll learn to travel in time with my own body." He ignored the picture of a headshake. "I don't care what you say. It may take me the rest of my life but I'm going to try."

The multi said: It's impossible.

Jack turned away.

Later, Jack was alone in the warm August night. He stood on the top terrace, under numbing stars, and slowly performed his movements.

I won't go there again, he thought. I will find the right Rachel in some world. Maybe in that world, but not at that time – I have used up my own memory, made an icon of it, just what I wanted to avoid.

I have to find the real Rachel.

I must learn, he thought, what happened then. That day.

The thought worried him.

18

It wasn't before Jack tried to travel into Rachel's consciousness that he understood the strength of the power preventing this.

The mind of another human. Another independent and unique human. It could simply not be done.

He wanted to. He tried. But he couldn't.

During many months, he'd gradually learned to stay in minds that in one way were his own, but in another not at all: other editions of him, in other worlds and lately in other times.

Somehow, he had imagined that he could make his way into another person's consciousness in that same way. Dreaming, trying, failing. Dreaming on and failing again. Feeling the first glimpses, overcoming the nausea. Learning to stay longer and longer. But always failing.

It had been easy to get into what had been versions of himself quite recently, a couple of months or a couple of years ago. The longer back he'd traveled, the worse the nausea had been. Still, he'd finally made it.

He knew that other people's psyches were quite different, different enough to harm him. But he wanted it to be possible. He tried to visit Rachel's mind.

The nausea didn't grow in him. It assaulted him. Struck him down and tossed him to the ground. He vomited violently. Although he knew that he had just barely brushed another human's consciousness, that he immediately had run away, he thrashed his arms and legs to break free.

When he got to his feet his white clothes were soiled. He was hyperventilating and his hands trembled.

A couple of hours later, he tried again.

Every attempt made it worse.

He gave in after the fourth or fifth try. His heart was beating very fast and quite irregularly. His pulse was rushing out of control; he didn't know if his heart would explode or just stop.

He tentatively stood up again. He wiped the worst clots from his clothes while the armadillos scuttled towards the mess on the ground.

Jack took of his clothes and gave them to his cleaning animals.

When he was feeling himself again, he walked in the young forest below the temple. The birches and spruce were more than fifteen feet high now, but they had grown quickly: they were still strangely thin and slender, almost like osiers. They moved lazily in the faint breeze.

Jack could see why experiments with telepathy had been abandoned.

He had brushed at a self that may have been Rachel's and immediately yanked back. No matter how much he wanted her, he wouldn't be able to make that kind of contact with her. He would never be able to get into her soul. The feeling was violently disgusting, like – he searched for similes – like eating your own lips, like trying to watch yourself by taking out your eye ... He couldn't find anything at all that even compared to the feeling of somebody else, *another*, meeting his mind and slithering around it, into it.

It was disgusting. Even though the other was somebody he loved.

After a few seconds, he threw up again.

He remembered his own simile about everybody blending into everybody else, gradually, like a person getting older. Obviously, the distance between him and Rachel was immense, like a five-year-old and a ninety-year-old. Possibly he might reach her, but overcoming the distance might take him centuries. Millennia.

He decided to try something else.

A couple of days went by before he could work again. He slept deeply, without dreams, as if his body and soul needed time to relax.

During the days, he walked in the forest and looked up at the temple and the slopes above it. One day he imagined re-building the slopes, making them as dramatic as the mountains behind Hatshepsut's original temple, but he didn't have the time.

First, he wanted to find Rachel. The real Rachel.

After that, he thought, he could enjoy himself by growing mountains. But first Rachel.

He realized he was recovering. And immediately traveled again.

$$\S$$

This time, traveling in his body was easier. Anything was easy, compared to what he'd just failed at. Jack worked and traveled: first short distances, then longer and longer.

He learned to go to other times and other worlds simultaneously. Now he could not only reach innumerable worlds in his own time, but any time in his own world; he could reach all times in all worlds.

The multiverse opened up to him. The feeling was intoxicating.

He remembered the stories from the Christian Bible, the ones that some colonists had mentioned. The ark, the crucifixion, the resurrection.

There were worlds where none of that had happened. But since all of it was possible, even the resurrection – Jack himself had traveled to worlds where he'd died earlier – there must be universes where all that had happened. Or where it was happening, right now.

Wrapped in white cloth, Jack saw Jesus being crucified. It was worse than he had expected. Jack didn't know very much about Christianity, but he remembered that Jesus was an aspect of God, born in human form.

The human part prevailed.

Jack stayed in the back as the man was nailed to the cross. He could hear Jesus saying something; the language was Aramaic and Jack couldn't make out one single word; all he heard was the feeble and lackluster tone. The dying man's panic was too overwhelming for his voice to work properly.

Later, when they raised the cross, Joshua ben Joseph's head hung limply down over his chest. His muscles couldn't hold it up.

The man whimpered, as feebly and piteously as when he'd spoken.

Jack let go of that world.

He saw the resurrected Messiah, too. It was impossible for him to decide if this was really happening, in the way Christians believed, or if the man with wounds in his hands and his side was someone who had traveled in the same way as Jack.

To Jack himself it would have been easy to study the living Jesus, to go back home again and modify his body to an exact copy, and to return on the third day after the crucifixion. Which meant that somebody must have done it.

Jack traveled back to the 20th century, to the city of Munich in Germany, where a little man with a rectangular mustache was gathering great throngs of followers.

Jack carried a methane handgun.

At first the thought of killing had seemed disgusting. But after a few seconds Jack realized that since it was possible for him to kill Adolf Hitler it had to happen, not just in one universe but in millions.

Which meant he might as well do it himself. Maybe the interference would change many more worlds.

He fired. The stinking gas filled the room. Adolf Hitler slowly toppled over while a dark spot widened on his brown shirt.

Men in similar shirts screamed and turned to Jack.

Jack let the rubber band tear him away.

He visited that same world, a century later, soon after the upheavals in his own world.

In the world where he had killed Hitler, the upheavals had never happened. Peace was everywhere and natural resources had been used judiciously. Jack wondered if the German dictator, one single person, really had been that important. He immediately realized that there were many worlds where this might not be the case. But in this world, Hitler's death had changed everything.

A dream world, Jack thought. There had to be other such worlds.

Maybe it was in that kind of world he would find Rachel.

Or maybe his love was in the most torn and tormented of all worlds.

Jack saw Hiroshima and Nagasaki annihilated. He was in one of the towers in old New York when the airplanes came roaring. He was in Rome in 2028, when the four young men sneaked in their stolen nuclear warhead.

He heard Abraham Lincoln speak at Gettysburg, felt the scorching heat in Dresden in 1945, saw Laurence Olivier as Coriolanus in 1938; he saw the American president's head yank backwards in Dallas 1963 and Apollo 11 being launched six years later.

He wanted to find Rachel. But he also wanted to experience his world. And worlds around it.

He saw Stalin's speech after the peace treaty in 1959, saw Lee Harvey Oswald captured a minute before the motorcade passed, saw the first Mars expedition land in 1999. He saw the world happy and unhappy, rich and poor, empty and crowded. And of course he traveled to Deir el-Bahri to see, just once in his life, the death temple of Queen Hatshepsut in all its splendor, newly built and ornamented, dazzlingly white under the merciless sun. The sight filled him with emotions without names. Afterwards, he kept traveling, on and on, visiting a vortex of worlds. But something had begun growing in him; something that filled him and took him over.

It was time to search for Rachel again.

Jack dreamed. He sat in a deck chair on the enamel and felt the heat against his skin. Let his thoughts fly to a thousand different worlds.

He must be able to do it. It had to be possible. Because he could imagine it and no logic made it impossible.

What he wanted to do was to go to a world where he already existed. He wanted to spy at himself and Rachel, to see what had really happened.

As far as he knew, this was impossible. But he could imagine it and so, it had to happen.

He had traveled mentally and visited himself. But only himself. Or he could travel with his body; but not to a world where he already was.

He dreamed until he had an inkling of a solution.

He sunk down. Further and further down. And then he knew.

§

He contacted his son. Joss, the man with a lynx's face.

"Yeah," Joss said over the net, "I've got backups."

"But none here?"

"In the temple? No."

Jack explained what he wanted and his son accepted.

My biological son, Jack thought. They had no relationship at all. Under the cat's face, Jack thought he could glimpse his own features. But young Joss meant nothing to him.

Except that he might be able to help Jack.

The body was in a big tank of enamel. There were valves for nutrition and waste.

Jack opened the tank and looked at the body. A lynx face. Paws with retractable claws instead of feet.

The body was alive, biologically speaking. But its mind was empty.

Jack was going to try something that he had never heard of. He would place his own consciousness in one of his son's backups. This was possible since the body had never been used. No other mind had sullied its autonomous functions.

Jack connected himself and uploaded his consciousness into it.

He did this without switching off the mind in his own body.

He awoke within minutes. The confusion and uncertainty were worse than when he traveled to Shylock and back. He didn't know all his muscles and his reflexes were quite a lot faster than he was used to.

"Hi," the man sitting next to him said.

From his lynx' eyes, Jack studied himself.

Their conversation was short. At the moment when Jack woke in the modified body, they had exactly the same memories and the same plans. Very few words needed to be said.

The Jack with a human body didn't stay for long. The modified Jack thought that this resembled the telepathy experiments. He himself felt queasy when he saw the man in the human body. Something was way too close, somehow embarrassing, awkward.

Jack with the human body left. He walked down towards the young forest. The modified Jack watched him and knew that he would be strolling there. Impatiently waiting.

Feline Jack learned his new body. He immediately discovered the advantages of cat genes: his sight and hearing were many times sharper. Before, he had seen a dot in the sky, far away. Now he could identify a peregrine. If the bird came closer, he could hear its wing strokes.

The world was sharper, more defined. A green blur in the distance became distinct patterns of leaves.

He traveled. He practiced a few times, made short trips, visited different worlds, saw himself in them. Went further and further back.

He had a plan.

The body he inhabited wasn't his own. On the other hand, his thoughts and memories were. But his lower reactions, in the limbic system and brain stem, were different: largely untainted by human consciousness.

He was Jack but still not. This ought to make it possible for him to exist in a world where he already was.

He avoided days and was very careful at night. The time he visited was about twenty years before his night with Rachel, but the place was the same.

He saw Rachel's father and his workers build the house. His new senses were amazing; he could be far away and still hear every word, see every expression.

When the house was ready, Jack knew everything about it, every room, every corridor and door. He knew where the windows were and how he could make his way to the attic or to the cold alcoves. During nights after feasts, when everybody was fast asleep, he dared to sneak around the house on his soft paws. He wrapped himself in dark fur to not be seen; if somebody had seen him, he would pretend to be an animal; but this never happened.

He traveled quickly, just a few short trips, through thirteen years. He saw Rachel grow up, saw her get her own room and learned everything about that. He carefully memorized the doors and windows nearby.

He also learned everything there was to know about the workers' cottage where he himself had lived.

All this was done in just a couple of days. Now and then he'd returned to his temple to eat and rest. He saw his human form a few times at a distance, one or two times nearby. The two nodded politely at each other but nobody had anything to say.

At last, he was ready.

In his lynx-like body, Jack waited in the forest. He saw Rachel coming there; she seemed excited and bright, almost giggly. She waited until the young Jack, not quite steady, approached his cottage.

"Jack!"

It all happened again.

He avoided spying on the couple during the night. At first he had intended to do that, but the thought made him queasy and he was unspeakably embarrassed by seeing himself making love. Also, he didn't like his looks: this was the original Jack, before he had met the multi. He left his peephole and waited in the woods.

Dawn came and Rachel left the cottage.

The modified Jack followed her.

It was as he'd suspected.

§

She went into the main building. Jack sneaked in by climbing to the roof and making his way into the attic. He had prepared his chinks and peepholes and saw her walking along the corridor.

She didn't go into her own room. She went on.

To the room where Max lived.

Jack sneaked across the beams in the attic until he was above Max's room. There was only one narrow chink, by one of the cornices. For a moment, Jack considered going back a few years and creating a better opening.

He didn't have the serenity to do that. He needed to know. Now.

The dark-haired girl softly entered the room. The curtains weren't properly drawn and the morning sun made its way in. Max was fast asleep, snoring and naked; he'd thrown his blanket off.

Rachel silently doffed her cape. And the rest of her clothes.

She got into the bed, next to Max. Max moved. Rachel giggled and jostled him with her shoulder. He opened his eyes.

"What?"

"Move over," Rachel whispered. "I'm here now."

"I want to sleep."

"You can't."

Her lips found his nipple. Max opened his eyes again.

Jack's lynx-modified heart beat violently.

She went straight, he thought, straight from my bed to his.

This time, he couldn't stop watching.

Straight from my bed, Jack thought again. To his.

Something roared in him, a visceral storm; he could feel his lips drawing back and claws emerging. He wanted to kill.

Afterwards, the couple spoke softly. Jack was both thankful for his sharp predator's hearing and in despair about it.

It didn't matter, he thought, still with his sharp claws digging into the heavy beam. If he hadn't caught their words now, he would have found a way and returned here again.

He had to know. However unendurable the pain was.

"You fell asleep," she said, her voice teasing.

"I drank too much," the young man next to her murmured.

They were naked and sweaty. Rachel lay with one leg across Max's thigh. Max's eyes were closed and he seemed to want to sleep.

"Don't drink too much."

"Well, I did."

She tickled his back. He moved impatiently.

"Stop it."

"You fell asleep," she said again. "So I had to enjoy myself in another way."

Max didn't seem to mind.

"With Love?"

"Not with Love," she said.

He opened one eye and smiled drowsily. "Jenny? Interesting."

"Not," she said, "Jenny."

Max turned his head to watch her. "So who?"

"Guess." Rachel's smile was delighted.

Max thought. He shrugged.

"No idea." He closed his eyes again.

He's totally uninterested, Jack thought above them. Totally uninterested.

This has happened many times before –

"Jack," she said.

"Jack?"

"The foreman. The young guy. The one who's been checking me out. You know."

"You're out of your mind," Max said listlessly.

"Well, he was interested, anyway. And not too drunk."

"Your father's going to kill you if he hears."

Rachel said, "He'll never hear."

The conversation cut into him like knives. His claws dug even deeper into the beam, his throat desperately wanted to growl, but Jack couldn't stop listening.

The worst thing, he realized in a while, wasn't that Rachel had gone straight to Max. The worst wasn't even that she spoke carelessly of Jack – "Well, not bad," she said, "but nothing I'll care to remember."

The worst was why she did this.

She described details from the night to excite Max. Before long, they were having sex again.

Jack's keen eyes showed him everything. He saw the joy in her eyes, the joy that he had carried with him so long, and realized that he had misinterpreted it: he had imagined that her joy had something to do with him, but it was quite as big now, or bigger, and Jack realized that her joy was only for herself, for her youth, her beauty, about what her body could do with men and what it could make men do with her. Jack had been a night's entertainment but hadn't meant more to her than a dinner course, a glass of wine.

Something that had been at hand. Filling in for Max.

Hidden in the attic, Jack breathed heavily, jerkily, more or less in time with the couple below him but for quite different reasons.

He stayed all the way to the end.

He had to be sure. Confirm what he already knew.

Rachel went to her own room just before the house began waking up. She chose new clothes and went down into the basement to shower.

The lynx Jack hid nearby. He waited.

When breakfast was already laid out, Rachel went to see her father. Matti sat on one of the terraces, eyes closed against the morning sun.

"I have to see you about something," Rachel said.

"Yes?"

"That Jack. The foreman."

"So?"

Matti looked up.

"Nothing strange about that."

"He made me ... made improper suggestions," she said demurely.

A piqued virgin. She cleared her throat before going on. "I don't want him here."

Matti nodded. He touched her hand. "I'll talk to the supervisor right after breakfast."

"Can't you do it now? Please?" The shy virgin became a pouting little girl.

Her father nodded and got to his feet.

All lies, Jack thought. All fake. Acting.

She used me. And I fell for it. Head over heels.

His throat was silent, his claws retracted. Beaten. He apathetically let himself fall back to his own time.

Jack connected his modified body to a memory bank by nerve fiber. As soon as he was done, he called for his human counterpart.

The human Jack watched him. His eyes grew worried.

"Not good?"

"Not at all. Let me sleep."

The human Jack emptied the lynx's brain.

Jack downloaded the memories and his heart sank. He closed the storage tank over the lynx's body with its empty brain and turned on the nutrition; he didn't know if his son would ever use this body, but he acted automatically. Still mechanically, he contacted his son to collect the body.

Via the net, he looked into the face that had just fallen asleep, free of all thoughts and memories, falling into oblivion. The feline face was peaceful. Jack wished he had been the lynx.

"How'd it go?" Joss said.

"As I deserved."

Rachel wasn't who he'd believed her to be.

He cursed himself for not guessing this earlier – or, rather, not letting himself guess. All the signs had been there: he had seen her flirting with many ever since he came to the farm, seen her with Max, then with Love, then with Max again, but he hadn't wanted to admit it to himself.

It had taken him seven centuries. But now he knew.

She had never been the person he'd thought.

He thought of all the clues he had had. The slavery world. The world of Satan worship. Even here in his own world, the world where Jack had first met her, there had been a kind of slavery. And Rachel had been born into a class that used workers or slaves.

He couldn't remember anything she'd done or said that hinted at her disliking the system.

He sat on the enamel terrace, looking out over his expanses. Far away, a herd of reindeer moved. The animals were blurry and vague for his human eyes. Jack idly wondered if he owned them.

That didn't matter. The temple and all his riches didn't matter at all.

§

Self-reproach came.

I should never have done that, he thought. It was rash. He who eavesdrops must be prepared to hear unpleasant things about himself; that happened to me and I only have myself to blame.

Now, I don't even have my dream.

He thought about the multiverse. About the fact that there were billions of Rachels, who were exactly the girls he wanted. Who had gone to their own beds right after their night with him, who awakened and had been told that Jack had been sent from the farm, that had stayed in their rooms, quietly weeping all day, face in their pillows.

They existed. But that couldn't help him. He wanted that very Rachel he'd been with that night. Yes, he thought, I'm quite aware that this is verging on madness. But she was the one I was with that night, and if I found somebody else – a Rachel that changed her mind afterwards, maybe as soon as I'd left the farm, crying in her pillow for weeks, or maybe a Rachel that was with me that night because she actually cared for me – even if I were to find somebody like that, I'd know that she wasn't really the one I loved, and like that one with the shrill laugh, I'd sneak out. I'd sneak out in the night, being the jerk I am, and keep dreaming hopelessly.

Now, it seemed, even his dream was gone forever.

19

Finally, he thought: This is enough. I can't keep wasting my life this way, year after year, body after body.

He was still stunned. Days went by as he just sat, immovable, high in his temple, unseeing eyes resting on the forest growing below. His thoughts had ground to a halt. Only at intervals, something glimmered.

His thoughts slowly began working again. One day, he thought about history being full of cuckolded lovers. But nobody before him had needed seven centuries to understand what had happened.

Other strange ideas and concepts quickly flew or slowly crept by. I could try to create my own Rachel, he thought. Use my gift for modifying genomes: visit some edition of her, somewhere in the multiverse, collect her DNA and grow her in a tub of cornea. Program her during all her childhood and adolescence, kiss her and dream her.

But no. He quickly discarded this thought. Aside from the unpleasant thought of raising another person for the single purpose of becoming his lover, he could never trust the love of such a person: she would be a creature that he himself had created, a kind of Frankenstein's monster.

And loving your own creation, he had heard somewhere, was only self-love of a kind.

He wanted a Rachel that loved him of her own free will. Someone who was, to the smallest detail, the one he dreamed of. He knew she was there, in billions of editions, somewhere in the multiverse. But if he would finally find her, he thought, if he actually would find exactly the Rachel he wanted – wouldn't she feel like his own creation even then? As if he had dreamed her, created her by his own will? He knew he was harping on the same string, thinking the same old thoughts, stuck in loops that might be centuries old. Over and over again, never seeing even the faintest glimmer of a way out.

It was hopeless.

At long last, he began taking his walks again. He went up to the rapids and let the roaring water numb him. The water had roared here for thousands of years and would probably go on for thousands more.

Nobody knew how long you could live by changing bodies over and over again. One day, maybe you got tired and wanted to sleep.

He could imagine throwing himself into the raging water.

No, he realized, his sons would give him a new body again. They or somebody else. He hadn't backed his memories up since he found out the truth about Rachel. Maybe he would search again, have to live through that morning again. And if he made a backup and got a new body, what good would that do him?

Of course, he might instruct his sons to destroy his bodies, burn his memories, never wake him. He was sure they wouldn't mind. They would inherit all he had.

That alternative felt better. But he didn't have to decide. Not yet.

His walks grew longer. As he wandered in the tundra above the rapids and saw lichen clinging to the ground, he sank into dreams again. The dreams were always the same, showing Rachel and Max. Although his senses were less keen now, the vivid memories remained: he would see what Rachel and the boy had done, hear them whisper; his keen sense of smell had even separated their breaths.

He wanted to stop but couldn't.

And with time, as the days followed each other, his memories slowly grew less painful. Like all other memories they were ground down and diluted by mixing with other recollections; defenses that he gradually invented; comparisons with other experiences; sensual impressions like warm winds, the hot sun, hunger or aching feet. The very persistence of his remembrance wore down its sharp points into something blunt.

The pain remained but he got used to it.

He avoided the thought of visiting other worlds again. Slowly, gradually, he felt another solution brewing within him.

Others had lost loved ones and survived. Jack had lived for seven centuries, ten normal human lives. He ought to be able to live for at least that long again. If a dismissed and lass-lorn bachelor in the seventeenth century had been able to forget his despair and go on with his life, Jack should also be able to.

He had traveled in thousands of worlds and times but actually never seen or learned very much. The search for Rachel had obsessed him to such a degree that he only remembered glimpses. Snapshots: slavery, beautiful scenery, strange buildings. A thousand worlds hadn't given him anything.

But his own world remained.

He got in touch with Joss, who promised that either he himself or Ben would take care of the temple. He refreshed his body, started jogging instead of walking, exercised and meditated. The images of Rachel and Max still haunted him but slowly slid to the background.

Only some nights he suddenly sat up in his bed, those memories burning in his mind, and thought that his own faint whimper had woken him.

He packed, carefully choosing clothes and other things. The trip would be long.

Winter was coming when the bioplane arrived to pick him up. Joss wasn't there yet, but that didn't matter. Jack nodded to the pilot and sat as far back as possible, alone in the cabin.

As the plane took off, he looked out over the temple. White rectangles shone against autumnally dark stone and black tree branches. He saw the temple shrink behind him and thought about how the enamel would one day yellow and crumble.

But not yet, he told himself. His body was young and strong and he was embarking on the journey of his life.

He would learn his world.

§

He flew to the Orient, to countries that had been called Iran and Iraq and Saudi Arabia when he grew up. Large sections of the old deserts were now covered by palms and modified grass. Caravans swayed along or made camp by streams. He saw the area between the Euphrates and Tigris, one of the places where the Garden of Eden was said to have been: an Arab prince had built the garden according to all the descriptions in the Old Testament and the Qur'an, making it as real as it could be. The gates were guarded by cherubim with four faces and a flaming sword. In the garden itself, you could see the serpent, crawling on its belly; anyone who wanted to might undress, go naked, and let the serpent tempt them; the fruit of the tree that was in the middle of the garden, a modified apple tree, smelled lovely and most people let themselves be tempted. Jack met an Eve, not at all modified, from old France and let himself be tempted with her, and by her. A dazzling God appeared, banishing them from the garden, and they laughed heartily when they dressed outside the gates.

"You do believe in this?" the woman said. Her name actually wasn't Eve but Marie-Claire.

Jack smiled. "Hardly."

"Me neither. But it was fun, no?"

They spoke English and liked each other's company. Close to the garden was a Hotel Babel, an enormous tower, which Marie-Claire pointed out was hundreds of miles from old Babylon. They didn't let this bother them. They spent a wine-drenched evening together and Jack let himself be seduced. But he thought of Rachel, all along he thought of Rachel, and as soon as Marie-Claire breathed deeply and slowly, he sneaked out of her room.

He went further south, to Africa. The mountain Kilimanjaro had lost its snow before Jack was born, and the area around the equator was still unbearably hot: he saw apathetic people basking in the sun, fanned by modified butterflies. National parks overflowed with tourists, many of them with feline traits. In the parks were original lions and leopards and sometimes it was hard to tell the humans apart from them. It all felt indolent and stale and Jack flew on.

He went to the southernmost point of mainland South America, began in Tierra del Fuego and worked his way north. At what had been the Petite Moreno glacier in Argentina, he saw the gauchos riding around their herds, all men, all dressed in lace and silk. None of them were feline. One of the men, dark-skinned and young and called Felipe, spoke to him and suggested that he stay for a while. Jack took him up on his offer and learned to ride.

The work was hard. All they could do at night was rest. Nobody was there for the money: someone followed a family tradition, others liked the physical work.

They had Sundays off. Those days, they rode into a small town by Lago Argentino to flirt with girls. Felipe disappeared with a Teresa and Jack was eagerly courted by a black-haired Luz. He politely declined and then tossed and turned all night: Luz and Rachel mixed, melted together and divided again, in his dreams.

He stayed for about a month. The weeks were okay but the free Sundays got to him. As soon as he wasn't exhausted, Rachel grew like a shadow in him. On the fifth Sunday he said goodbye to Felipe and left.

§

He saw the Inca city Machu Picchu, hidden between two steep mountains, and wondered at people having lived there. On his way towards the Pacific, he flew over the enormous pictures that some-body had created on the ground. He seemed to see modified animals and humans and wondered if multis had been involved.

He didn't call for the multi. He wanted to travel alone, giving himself time to grind down the blunt pain even more.

He couldn't decide if he wanted to go to Easter Island or continue north to see the Aztec temples in Mexico. At last, he tossed a coin, decided to go to Easter Island, and his life changed again.

Some of the stone sculptures were thirty feet high. Jack walked among them. The sun burned down, high in a deep blue sky, and made the hatchet faces throw hatchet shadows. It was incredibly hot. Jack had placed himself in the shadow of one statue to cool down when he saw the woman.

Rachel, he thought.

No.

It was Liya. She glanced uncertainly at him.

§

The coincidence was strange. There were almost five billion people on Earth. Although many of them enjoyed traveling, few took the trouble to go to Easter Island. Even fewer stayed for more than a couple of hours; just a moment before he saw her, Jack had decided to go back to his plane.

If he'd left a few moments earlier he would have missed her. If she'd arrived a little later, he would have been gone.

He thought about the multiverse but immediately discarded the notion.

She wasn't modified at all. She looked just like she had done during their training.

"Do you recognize me?" he said.

She hesitated. "... Jack?"

"Jack."

She smiled and her eyes immediately enchanted him.

This is Liya, he admonished himself. He was irritated with himself when Rachel appeared in him. This is Liya, not Rachel. This girl has never let you down. And although she looks like Rachel, she has other qualities.

"So you didn't die on Shylock?" she said.

They sat in an air-conditioned bar down by the tourist harbor. Biological planes and boats in all shapes and colors lay on the glittering water. Liya drank coffee. Jack had ordered Scottish single malt.

He felt like he needed that.

"I went home," he said. "After just a local year. Veen – you remember? – Veen got tired of the place. I was torn between going with him and staying with you."

"So we were together?"

This was the third time she asked.

"We were together," he assured her for the third time. "A few months."

"And I wanted to have children with you."

He nodded.

"Was that why you went? To escape?"

"I don't know," he said, neither really lying nor being quite truthful. "I never really liked Shylock. The place was bleak. The sun and atmosphere made everything brown and dark red. We slaved for months to find minerals for farming. For a while, food was rationed."

"And then it all broke down."

None of them remembered that happening. Liya's only memories were of training for the expedition. Jack had left Shylock before its biology ran amok, filling the colonists' lungs with ferns. All he and Liya knew was what they had found on the net.

When she woke after leaving for Shylock, Liya had expected to have a new body. Instead, she awoke on Earth, in a body impossible to tell from her previous one.

Jack was the first colonist she had met since then.

"Maybe nobody wants to see anybody else," she said. "When I came to, Peter and Sara were still in that amniotic fluid. I could have waited a few days but I didn't want to. Nobody else had waited."

"And I haven't tried to see anybody."

"What have you been doing? You've been back for years."

He said, "Traveling."

They talked all evening. After more whisky, and after Liya had had some wine, they were both very glad that they'd met. After a dialogue with quite a lot of subtext undertones, they decided to share a room. The hotel was supposedly full but Jack bribed the manager.

Naturally, they had sex.

To Jack this was familiar, a renewal of something they'd done many times before. To Liya, the experience was totally new. She cried afterwards and Jack held her until they slept, thinking about her experience – making love to somebody who was completely new to you, but who knew all your triggers, when to do what and how to do it.

Jack woke. During the first half-conscious seconds, he didn't know where he was. He saw the dark-haired woman beside him and became, for just a few moments, a wave function oscillating between Matti's farm and Liya in her hut, between now and then, between Earth and Shylock. The multiverse brushed at him but he pushed it away and let the waveform collapse. He accepted where he was; and with whom.

"Fly with me to Mexico City," he said.

They had breakfast in a large and sunny room, overlooking the nearest statues. The food was better than Jack had expected and the night had given him a voracious appetite.

She watched him. That uncertain glance again.

"Why?"

"Why not? Where are you going?"

"Nowhere," she said. She stirred her coffee to avoid his gaze. "Everywhere. But ..."

"It wouldn't have to mean anything." He hesitated, trying to find the right words. "I'm very glad I met you. Things went awry between us on Shylock but that doesn't have to mean anything either. We were other people there."

"What if things go wrong again?"

He shrugged. "Would that make anything worse? We've lived without each other for hundreds of years. We can live without each other for hundreds of years more. I just think –", he tried to find words again – "I just feel it would be interesting to travel a little together. Maybe a few days, maybe longer. See what happens."

She considered. Then she said, "No."

He flew alone to Mexico City, found his way to Tenochtitlan and studied the enormous step pyramids. They reminded him of his own temple, the Egyptian queen's death temple, but the associations were different: here, heads and other body parts had been thrown down by Aztec priests to appease the gods of a culture so obsessed with death that it waged constant wars to capture enough prisoners to sacrifice. Jack made it all the way up the steps to the great platform of Templo Mayor and looked out at the ruins. He tried to imagine what it had been like when hundreds of people were sacrificed but didn't feel anything in particular.

The reaction came when he'd left Tenochtitlan. He was feeling queasy; the multiverse whispered to him again and he realized that there were worlds where the gory sacrifices still happened, now, at this moment, himself both executioner and victim in different universes. He found a modern hotel, as far from the pyramids as possible, and went to sit in the bar. When he waved to the bartender for tequila, he met Liya's gaze.

"I changed my mind," she said.

He said, "So I see."
She sat next to him. Her large eyes were uncertain.
"Don't let me down."
He said, "Never."

They traveled together. Liya was his guide in the Hawaiian isles, but Jack could see why she had left her native country; not just the relentless heat, but especially the indolent, pakalolo-smoking and holo-consuming people, gave him a feeling of listlessness. They went on to Japan and saw one of the first genome cities, a manga fantasy created by Kawanabe and Kanagaki just decades after the multis had taught humanity how to modify DNA. Improbable buildings climbed in and over each other, still alive and growing after centuries, slowly sliding up and down, in and out, to create new and always surprising shapes. The city was a labyrinth with no solution. You could walk in a corridor, turn around to go back and find that the corridor had disappeared, or divided into three. Jack and Liya spent an entire day trying to understand the layout but ended up almost a mile further south than they'd thought. They laughed at their mistakes at a dinner with ersatz geishas and rice wine and then made love, slowly and tenderly, in a suite far above the churning city. Afterwards, Jack lay awake. He thought, I could live like this.

They went on. They saw the Forbidden City in Peking and the half-living, slowly marching copy of the Terracotta Army before they went north to the new enamel sections of the Wall and the fields of modified rice. Impressions succeeded each other and sometimes there were several hours when Jack never thought of Rachel.

But she tried to come back. Jack's gaze could become distant at some dinner table and Liya worried.

"What are you thinking of?"

"Oh, nothing."

"Sure?"

He smiled at her, thankful that she'd brought him back. "I'm so glad you're here."

This was true. He actually was happy that she was with him.

But sometimes he wondered why.

They traveled west through Asia. Siberia wasn't the cold tundra Jack had seen in holos when he was a boy. Now, thick forests grew everywhere, apple trees, coconut palms and new designed fruits, while mammoths, created from genes of frozen bodies, wandered in great herds. Jack and Liya kept going west and were dazzled by the sun glittering in Lake Baikal, landed on the grass steppe and saw horsemen get drunk on fermented mare's milk. Jack tried to be attentive to Liya, every day, every minute.

He suspected that she could feel that. That he was trying.

"You don't have to make efforts for me."

"I don't."

"You have no responsibility for me."

"But I care for you."

"Promise?"

They were staying in Istanbul, close to the replica of Hagia Sophia, when he had a long dream of Rachel. In his dream she was compliant and tender and asked him to forgive her, said that she had been young then, that she had been playing with both Jack and Max but that now, she was sorry.

That she wanted Jack to live with her.

Jack woke from his own ragged breathing. Liya was fast asleep beside him.

The multiverse brushed at him again.

He tried to hide it, but he guessed she suspected something.

"Am I a burden to you?"

No, he wanted to say, far from it. You are saving me. You are my only protection.

He couldn't tell her that. It would immediately make her feel that he actually didn't want her – that he was using her. And of course, she would be right.

The dreams came more and more often, just like on Shylock. They were like a curse. A dark cloud hanging over Jack.

He became even more attentive. He listened to every word she said, let her decide everything, from their next destination to dinner drinks, never allowed himself to get lost in dreams. After a couple of days she said, "What's going on with you?" and he said that he loved her.

He had said this on Shylock, but never before on Earth. He could tell it made her happy. And he believed that it was true. She was bright, wise, funny and beautiful; when she decided something, he always knew she was right.

The days became better and better. But there were nights, too.

One night, on a Greek island, Jack dreamed of Shylock. He had had similar dreams before, seen biology run amok and cover the planet, trailing across streams and hills in one of the countless developments making up the universe. This time, the dream was tinted by the living manga city. Jack walked in gliding corridors, waiting for somebody. He didn't want to know who, tried to get out of the dream, but she kept coming closer. He could feel her right behind him, he suddenly knew who she was, he both wanted to and didn't want to turn and then he felt Rachel's arms around his neck.

He woke, not really knowing if the dream had been a nightmare or something he wanted to return to. He was about to close his eyes again when he glimpsed something in the dark room. Liya was awake. She sat next to him, legs crossed in the lotus position.

"Who is Rachel?" she said.

Afterwards, he regretted that he didn't tell her. And, he went on, if it hadn't happened in that very moment, if it hadn't happened just when he was midway between dreaming and waking, touched by the multiverse, if he had had time to think it over, he would probably have told her.

As it was, he didn't.

"Rachel?" he said.

"You said it in your sleep."

He shrugged. "No idea." And then he rolled over to her. "Come here."

They went on into Europe. On the surface, nothing had changed, but Jack kept seeing the pictures over and over again.

You are a fool, he told himself. You are traveling with a wonderful woman, everything should be lovely, but you can't let go of the thought of a spoiled girl who toyed with you one night seven centuries ago and then threw you away. Literally; she let somebody else take care of it, but it was she who actually threw you out. Like leftover food or old clothes. She had her fun with you one night when she couldn't find anyone better and then she let you go. Forget her, forget her now.

And he suddenly realized that he himself, to Liya in countless universes, was as spoiled and inexplicable as Rachel was to him:

that there had to be billions of worlds where Liya tried to find him, obsessed with their time on Shylock or other times they'd spent together, without finding the Jack she wanted. I have to pull myself together, he thought, before this time, our trip together, becomes another such encounter – an encounter that makes Liya hunt me through the multiverse, to make her hopeless dreams true.

He thought about this over and over again but couldn't make himself do anything. The multiverse grazed him, more and more often. Their days darkened.

"You were dreaming of her again."

"Who?" he tried.

"Rachel. You whispered her name."

"Can't remember."

Liya bit her lip. "Who was she?"

"Nobody."

And so, he missed yet another chance to tell her. This would happen again, and again. While they neared old France he tried to outdo himself in being attentive, listening, being with her in the moment. In a good mood, full of fun. Showing her his love.

But his dreams were returning.

Liya grew quiet. Now, it was her eyes that became distant; it was her not hearing what Jack said.

"Sorry?"

"I was just wondering. What you're thinking of." He tried to smile.

"Same as you."

"What?"

"Do I have to spell it out?"

One morning in Paris, just a few blocks from the place where the Eiffel Tower once had stood, he woke alone in their hotel suite. He called for her but Liya didn't answer. Jack got out of bed. The door to the bathroom was open.

Liya's bags were gone.

There was a note on the coffee table.

I'm sorry. I tried. I couldn't make it.

You're dreaming of somebody else. You have to find her. Your Rachel. Whoever she is.

I don't want to be in your way.

I don't want to hear you murmuring her name in bed, just minutes after we've made love.

I wish you well. I'm sorry.

He stood naked at the coffee table. The first thing he felt was relief.
Now he could search for Rachel again.

20

Before he was home in his temple again, he'd made up and changed his mind twenty times over. He would spend the rest of his days finding his one perfect Rachel; nothing else mattered; his new attempt to live with Liya proved how that relationship was impossible and how Rachel would always appear in his dreams. And then: No, never, he'd wasted centuries by chasing an impossible dream. It was time to get his act together. He'd tried thousands of times with Rachel and at least two with Liya. Liya had to be the one he needed.

And then: Why would he need anybody? Why not try finding himself instead of chasing meaningless dreams? What man or woman could be enchanted by someone blurting out "You're my everything, I can't live without you ..."

He decided. And changed his mind again.

When the white rectangles of the temple glittered at him from gray-brown spring land he was still uncertain. He shook hands with his lynx son. The plane took off and disappeared.

Jack went into the temple. Everything was the same, white enamel kept dazzlingly spotless by the anteaters. His sparse furniture.

All was quiet. He wasn't used to this silence after months in tourist towns and bustling cities. He stood still for a while and let the silence seep into him.

Below him, eighteen equally silent brains swam in their fluid. And in a few decades, it would be time to fill yet another one. To choose the memories to follow him in the next period of his life.

He thought: Rachel.

Jack's subconscious told him what he really wanted. What would happen.

He realized this when he was already walking out to the terrace to meditate. While he believed himself to be thinking about what he would do, the basic levels of his brain, together with the interference from billions of other universes, had already decided for him. His feet had started walking on their own accord.

It's a kind of addiction, he thought, passively trudging along. Like an alcoholic trying to control his drinking. Somebody addicted to drugs or sex or gambling and telling himself that he's in control as his feet are already carrying him toward the abyss.

I will stop, he thought. I will break free of this, find Liya, make her understand that I've finally changed; at last, I will find peace. But not quite yet.

Make me chaste. But not yet. I will try a couple of times more. Just to ...

He couldn't find an ending to the last sentence. He didn't need one.

He traveled again. This time, he combined time and space.

He imagined his night with Rachel, but in another universe; once again, he imagined different worlds as snapshots or holos, close to another in some unknown dimension.

Of course, he couldn't really see all those worlds. The pictures were just a way to visualize his dreams.

He flipped himself away from the night he had experienced, a few billion worlds to the side, he didn't know how many. Randomly chose one and traveled. The same night but in a different world, searching for the Rachel he dreamed of.

Everything was familiar until Anna gave up and left him at his table. For the first time, he wondered what had happened to her afterwards. She had said goodbye when he left the next day but after that, he had no idea.

It wouldn't have been too hard for him to find out. He just needed to visit the farm a few times; a few days later, a couple of weeks. A few years. He would have to grow a body, since he couldn't either bring his own or be inside someone but himself. But he could have found out what had happened to her. If he'd been interested.

After Anna left, he waited, by now familiar with small things that happened. In time, Rachel dragged the unsteady Max away. Jack waited a few minutes and then followed his younger body to the cottage.

There was no Rachel waiting at the edge of the forest.

Jack waited a little more. The naïve hope of the smitten, he thought. His body lay alone in its bed, not even closing its eyes, until the sun came in through the window. His younger body still staring at the ceiling, Jack gave in and let the weight throw him home.

So, just try again, he thought. And he did.

The next time, Rachel waited among the trees. Everything happened in the same way as in his own world until they were in his room. The door was yanked open. The supervisor and a worker dragged Jack out. He broke contact before anything else happened.

The third time, Rachel and Max left the party after less than an hour. Max was quite sober. They couldn't keep their hands off each other, kissing deeply even before they reached the main building. Jack emptily looked after them.

A few more tries. There was no Rachel there; Anna refused to leave Jack, no matter how rude he was to her; the feast was interrupted when Matti fell ill; or when there was a fire in the main building; or when something stuck in Love's throat and he almost died. And so on.

Jack realized that he needed help. He called for the multi.

What you're doing isn't good for you, the multi told Jack after listening to him. You're hollowing your soul.

"I can't stop," Jack said.

Nobody else can choose for you. I can give you advice, but I can't tell you what to do.

Jack thought.

"The worst of it is," he said, "that it doesn't matter anymore. I've tried thousands of times. I know that the probability of succeeding is close to zero. But it's like it doesn't even matter anymore if I succeed or not. It's the thrill. There is something in the very act of trying, the new attempt that I've never done before, that is thrilling in itself. Do you see?"

What you're describing isn't uncommon in humans, the multi said.

"At the same time, it feels more and more ... hollow. Empty. The only moments that matter are those when I choose the next universe. It's a kind of kick, a quick rush of adrenalin and endorphins, I guess. But in a few seconds, it's over and everything is empty again."

True. But it's your own choice.

Jack wasn't listening. "And I'm getting this silly picture in my head. The power that pulls me home to my own world, you know, the one feeling like a rubber band? I've begun imagining that the rubber band might snap. That the power, whatever it might be, will suddenly end and I'll roam in millions of worlds without ever finding my way home again. I know it's ridiculous, but it feels like that could happen. And whatever can happen also will happen, somewhere ..."

The multi didn't answer.

"Am I right?"

It sounds possible, the multi said presently. Conceivable. An infinitesimally small possibility. Which means that it is there.

"So I should stop."

Maybe not because of that. But you don't seem happy with what you're doing.

"No. And yes. I don't know."

The multi considered.

You think a lot, the multi's pictures said a few moments later in Jack's mind – you think a lot about finding a world where Rachel is the person you've been dreaming of. Since everything that is possible must happen, you know that there are multitudes of such Rachels. Versions of her, being the one you imagined, dreaming of you just like you've dreamed of her.

Jack nodded impatiently.

And in that case, there are also Rachels looking for you.

"And they will find me. A few, millions of them, will find me. But the one they find might not be – me. He might not be the one talking to you right now. And I only know me, I only have my own life within this bowl of bone." Jack tapped his finger on his temple. "I would try if I thought there might be a reasonable chance," he said. "But that waiting would be exactly like what I'm doing now. Quite as uncertain, or even more. And I wouldn't have any activity at all."

You prefer the rush.

"I prefer," Jack agreed, "having my rush."

The multi said: You will change your mind.

"What?" Jack was surprised. He straightened, staring at the blurred creature. "How do you know?"

We've spoken of this before, the multi said. But it's not that easy to understand.

Once again, the multi explained to Jack how every human followed his or her own track through the multiverse, how they moved from snapshot to snapshot because of their consciousness. Multis were different: they saw all possibilities, and all possibilities were equally real to them. The lives of humans were like choosing between products in a market; multis didn't have to choose but owned everything.

The multi went on.

Multis, it said, are the complete realization of almost everything that could happen to an individual, fuzzy and blurred as the copies of the individual were tall or short or fat – or as the countless copies slowly changed to other individuals. Every copy must follow its path; only the multi itself was the complete truth of a person

Jack nodded at this, not just because he could see the logic of it, but because the multi had just confirmed something he'd suspected for many months.

That was what I meant about humans falling through time, the multi said. And for you, this falling means that you will change your mind.

"Don't I have my free will?" Jack said aggressively.

Do you really? You know everything is interference and feedback. Even if we only consider this world, your own world, your personality is a result of other people that you've interacted with. Add the multiverse and everything becomes immensely more complicated. Years before the upheavals, researchers showed activity in the brain half a second *before* people thought they made decisions. What you believe to be you is a result of all your counterparts in the universe and everybody you've met on Earth. Just consider Rachel – would you have been the person you are today without her? Without Liya? Would Liya be who she is without you? Everything that happens, everything that makes you who you are, is caused by feedback and interference, in this world and others.

You are created the way you are, the multi said, this version of you has become who you are, and all your decisions will depend on that; you can be said to have free will, but we might equally well say all your decisions are predetermined. You do what you imagine that you've chosen, but in reality, you can't choose any more than a planet can choose its orbit. Everything already exists in the multiverse and the fact that you are the person you are makes you do what you do, even in the moments when you believe more than ever that you're rebelling; no matter how you try, you can't do anything but realize, complete, create yourself. With all the variations and variants there are throughout the multiverse.

Jack said, "And based on that, you know what I will do? That I'll change?"

Your path has been staked out.

Jack angrily shook his head.

He tried again, but the emptiness grew. Repeated attempts lead to all foreseeable results: Jack fell for Jenny on Shylock, Jack was attracted to Max instead of Rachel, Jack was the girl Jackie, finding herself being Rachel's rival ... And the attempts always ended in emptiness.

I could find Liya again, he thought for the thousandth time. Break free. Be better, act better towards her. Move in with her and live together.
But longing for the next rush already surged in him.

He kept searching, going further and further out through the elusive dimensions that were forking paths of the multiverse. Everything moved in circles: Rachel was too similar to the one in his own world, scornfully rejecting him; or she was too different, too dependent of him; or too merry, too sad, too tall, too short. Over and over again the circles repeated, until he found himself in worlds where Rachel was creatures he couldn't even describe. He returned to the temple as a diver coming up for air, breathing deeply and diving down again, chasing the kicks as much as he chased Rachel. Day or night didn't matter anymore.

He stopped walking, stopped washing, stopped eating except for grabbing a piece of bread or cheese. He no longer knew when he was dreaming, when he slept or when he traveled. His beard and hair grew and he lost weight. He became weaker. He was losing it. At last, he called for the multi again.

21

Have you changed your mind? the blurred shape asked. Jack couldn't even rise to his feet. He sat feebly at his table, supporting himself with his hands, trembling from cold and starvation.

"I don't know," he said.

Why did you call me?

"I don't know."

The multi gave him some kind of liquid food and let him sleep. When Jack woke, the creature stood by his bed.

"Have you waited here?"

And, the multi said, in ten billion other worlds.

"Why?" Jack said. "What do you want?"

The multi said: It's time you learned the truth.

As for everything and every living creature in the multiverse, the multi said, the versions of you must fulfill all your potential.

"I know this," Jack said. He was tired and exhausted. He felt numb and depressed.

This means that you have to live through all possible sequences of events in your life. There are versions of you that will find their Rachel. And others that never will.

You are in the latter group.

Jack sat up. The world keeled. "How do you know?"

You are in a group of universes where you will not find Rachel.

"Why haven't you told me before?" Jack almost stuttered. "Why, why did you let me –"

You weren't ready, the multi said. We know humans better than you think.

"I know. I know you're –"

The multiverse is a strange concept for humans and before you've experienced enough, you can't understand it.

Jack swallowed. "But you're saying I won't find her?" His breathing was ragged.

This copy of you won't. But there's more to this. You must have wondered who I am.

"You are a multi. The sum of an individual's copies across part of the multiverse."

True. But who is the individual?

Jack looked at the shimmering creature and sighed. "Well, you're me, who else would you be? I've known since –"

No, the multi said. You're wrong. I'm Rachel.

I can understand you guessing at yourself, the multi said. But still, I'm her.

"But how –?" Jack was confused.

You know the answer, multitudes of Rachel murmured to him. You have united your mind with yourself in hundreds of worlds, first ones most similar to your own, then more distant in every dimension. You know that the nausea is easily overcome in copies that are very nearly you; you have learned to overcome it and go further away. You should easily see how a long chain of Rachels, beginning anywhere, with the one you first thought you loved or with the dream you still are chasing, can be connected.

"You don't look like Rachel at all," he protested weakly. "You have no discernable form. You're too tall."

Because we live in the multiverse. I am a few million Rachels, or if you prefer, you can think of "me" as a window to millions of universes where Rachel exists. I am slim and small on some planets, tall and muscular on others; I move in different ways, and it all blurs together. All the individuals in the multi you're watching are both "here" and "not here." You first learned to travel with your mind and then with your body. We travel in a third way, by existing in a dream, a state where no individual makes conscious observations and no probabilities collapse; a state where millions of individuals can both be and not be in the same place. A state that you almost brushed at when you meditated in the sun and felt yourself travel.

Anyway, when my copies reached this state, we went back to your younger self and gave you the virus to modify DNA. The realization that your bodies weren't given for life prepared you for the multiverse: you could see the possibilities inherent in every human being. We did this long before you – "we," Rachels and Jacks and billions of others on the many worlds that developed the virus, learned to let go of our minds, to dream and travel, long before you did.

"Our genes," Jack said. "You said you wanted them. For your young."

The Rachel multi showed him a picture of a smile.

A white lie. A way of catching your interest. Would you have believed that I was Rachel? That you are parts of us?

§

Jack still felt stunned.

"You are Rachel," he said. "If you're Rachel, there must be a copy in you that is the one I'm looking for. One who wants me as I want her. Why haven't you led me to her?" He stared at the towering form. "Why don't you find her now? Rachel," he said, "you're in there, you can hear me, come to me, tell me where to go, show me the way ..."

The multi showed him the Rachel in his dreams, slowly shaking her head, a tear trickling down her cheek.

You still don't understand, the multi said. In a way, you're correct. But all the Rachels that make me up are dreaming now. They must, to create me, remember? Some of them may wake from the dream and feel wistful for you, others might laugh and shrug, but right now what you are talking to is the sum of Rachel. Her – and his – complete potential. And this being knows that all that can be, must be. Do you understand?

"I ..." He had no words.

I am, the multi said, an infinitely complex being. Since every living being in the multiverse morphs into every other, all borders are arbitrary. There are individuals that undoubtedly are you – or Rachel – although they live in a stone age or on one of Jupiter's moons in ten thousand years; there are others whose genes and lives obviously make them very like other people.

The borders between individuals are hard to draw. But the being talking to you right now is the Rachel who was born on Earth before the upheavals, who is still alive, if in different bodies, and whose life has been affected by your life and others in different ways – but in what you would consider to be the past: from our point of view, those things happened hundreds or thousands of years ago.

In a way, the multi went on, you can see me as the idea of Rachel. Every version of her, young and old, happy or devastated, man or woman or somewhere in between, alone on any planet, is just a pale copy of reality. The Rachel you dream of is what Plato's cave dwellers saw on their wall: a vague shadow of the truth. A phantom.

Reality is the sum of all the millions and billions of Rachel or Jack who realize all their potentials in as many worlds and times. The different versions might live in quite different times – born before the upheavals, during them or after; born a thousand years before, or in worlds where no upheavals ever happened – but the tendrils make it possible for them to contact each other, and others who are like them.

That's why multis have such a long now. And their now keeps expanding. The more Jacks that are connected by the threads to different copies, the more their world and time grows.

And as I said: some Jacks will have their Rachels, others not.

You belong to a group that will never find her.

"How do you know?" Jack repeated stubbornly.

He knew that his perpetual search for Rachel was the road to his ruin. But nobody, not even some superhuman version of Rachel herself, was going to tell him what he could or could not do.

The multi said: Because you are in a zone – let's call it a zone – of universes where it never happened.

"But I haven't given up!"

But you will. You are only one instance of yourself. You have thought of other possibilities – brushed at other versions of yourself – many times. Those versions exist. They have to exist. But you yourself, this version of you, must also exist. And together, you build a multi like me. Have built, will build.

And there's another reason why you have to stop.

The borders between individuals who are you and not-you are

fluid. There are worlds with men or with women who are exactly half you, half Rachel. It would be wrong to call them intermediate individuals. We might as easily see you, the individual I am talking to now, as an intermediate form between two other clearly not-Jack individuals.

You know this. In the multiverse, every individual morphs into everybody else. In a way, every individual *is* everybody else, since this is necessary to make everybody fulfill their potential. You might say the old pantheists were right: all is one. And of course, this is what makes telepathy and our melting together possible – one Rachel melts with another, very close to herself, then to the next, on and on and on.

At last, what was you and me will melt together with everybody else who ever lived. The borders between individuals and sexes will dissolve, then the borders between species; humans will first rejoin their astounding variants on colony planets, then their closest primate relatives, then other mammals; vertebrates will join invertebrates and echinoderms, mollusks, annelids and arthropods, limnognathia and sponges, cnidarians and comb jellies; they will join bacteria, fungi, grass and lichen, and in time also creatures that didn't emerge on Earth and that human brains can't imagine yet, until everything living has been united and the sum of possibilities is at last completed. As you may imagine an almost endless library, containing all the combinations that a small number of letters and punctuation signs can create, so the sum of DNA, too, creates an almost infinite totality. There is everything that you – all of you – and me and everybody else can be; and all is one; no time exists, since all time and all snapshots are united into one eternal moment.

Jack said, "You're saying you are God."

That's one way of putting it, the multi said. It's true that an almighty and all-knowing God is quite a remarkable metaphor for DNA's potential when it has been realized in a conscious universe.

"But a God has to be good."

Not at all, the multi protested. All potential must be realized. Both good and evil. A multiverse without suffering and evil wouldn't be complete. It would be a lie; and how could a lie be complete?

And this is why you must stop, will stop, trying to find your Rachel. You will realize that it is hopeless, and at last, you will find peace. When you have realized your destiny as a part of the multi Jack, you will join us. You will see clearly. You will be one with all the Jacks who found their Rachels. You will be one with all.

You, Jack, will be one of us. And we will be God.

Jack said, "Let's go out on the terrace. I need air."

They stood on the highest terrace, sun lavishly pouring glaring summer over the enamel surfaces, the multi like thin mist, then swirling white cloud, then, at the center, black and impenetrable.

"But," Jack said in a while. "But this only happens if I obey what you're telling me now. If I stop chasing my dream of her. What happens if I don't?"

In that case, the multi slowly said, the multiverse will not be consummate. You will make a choice that you shouldn't have made, and there will be a small flaw in the perfection. Which makes it impossible that you would act in that way.

"Why?" He felt like a stubborn child. But he had to know.

The multi said: Because the multiverse has to be complete. That is the definition of the multiverse: it's the sum of all particles and all their quantum states, raised to the power of themselves countless times. You might imagine the multiverse as a complete vacuum, at the same time impenetrably thick, of being and not-being. Every moment, every snapshot, every place in the multiverse is simultaneously full of nothing, of fire, of ice, of biological material in billions of versions; of living things and dead, of stars, planets, atmospheres and vacuum; of auroras, mist, smoke and dust; of moral tales and writings of harlots, of happiness and hate, smiles and sorrow. Everything is everywhere: all books possible to be written are written, all the potential existing in the particles of the universe, the letters of the alphabet or the letters of DNA, are layered over each other in that eternal moment.

So far, your life has been just falling through time, from snapshot to snapshot, mainly in one single trajectory. With a few short deviations since you began to fathom the multiverse. And like the universe where you were born is mainly empty – one light-second to the Moon, eight light-minutes to the Sun, thirty two light-years to Shylock, and in between, wastes of nothing – just like that, your life has mainly been empty; with a few fixed stars like your night with Rachel, those moments when you imagined you could be happy with Liya, and so on, a few other times which aren't in your head right now.

When you become one with us in the multiverse that emptiness will be gone. You will see the multiverse for real: the doors of your perception will be cleansed and you will see everything as it really is. The temple you have built here will be replaced by the temple of ultimate being. There will be no joy or sorrow that you don't experience in that eternal moment. All the possibilities existing for you, finding Rachel, losing her, owning all the world, losing everything, suffering, luxuriating, everything will be real for you at once. Rachel, the Rachel I am, will be a part of you and all your manifestations will be a part of her. And when you experience that, you will transcend good and evil. You will see infinity and realize that the dark colors are as necessary as the bright, cold as important as warmth.

You will finally understand.

How could you say no to something like that? To eternity?

And, the multi said after a short pause – if you do not accept, the multiverse will not be perfect. The little blemish will be there. The flaw in the diamond.

Jack considered. He was exhausted, worn to the bone and confused, but he tried to gather his thoughts and understand what the multi really said.

"You're saying," he croaked, then tried again. "You're saying that this edition of me, the one I think of as 'me,' lives in a zone of universes? And that all other copies of me in this zone change their minds?"

They give up, the multi said. They realize that they will never find the Rachel they want and they choose eternity instead.

"And since they do so, I must also do the same?"

Like a stone falls to the earth. Like a flower floats on water.

"But they don't always."

Like ice melts in heat.

For almost an hour, the sun reaching zenith and beginning its long descent, the multi tried to explain that Jack had no free will. Jack refused to agree.

"You can't know that," he said to the many Rachels trying to make him be like them. "You just take for granted that since the sun has risen every morning for billions of years, it has to rise tomorrow too. But that's wrong."

The multi flickered more than ever. The outer areas whirled wildly and even the black center seemed on the verge of dissolving. At last the creature's pictures said, more blurred than in years:

I know I'm right. To be certain, absolutely certain, is impossible. But statistically speaking it has to be so.

Jack said, "I've never believed in statistics."

At long last, the multi faded away. Jack slept, another long and dreamless night. In the morning he prepared a proper breakfast, the first in a long time. Summer was beginning and he could feel the scent of the forest below.

The slim trees were filling out, soon grown.

That's the scent of life, Jack thought while he squinted down at the green crowns. The sun stood right above the forest at this time of morning and Jack had no cat's eyes now. The trees blurred to a green carpet.

Life is being able to choose, he thought. No matter if this freedom is illusory – as long as you believe you have a choice, you will live according to that. But if you lose that freedom or even the illusion of it, what will be left? Only going through motions, following a fixed schedule. Never making mistakes and never feeling the rush of opportunities.

He straightened, closed his eyes in the sunlight and went on.

The multi wasn't Rachel. He could easily see that: the multi was all the instances of Rachel that he'd seen, and all he hadn't seen. In fact, he realized that if the multi was everything that Rachel could be, then it actually also was everything that he, Jack, could be. And everyone else – somewhere in the multiverse, everybody must be everything.

No individuality. No Rachel. All those Rachels had chosen to try to persuade him, but being composed of her, they weren't her. He didn't care.

Still, the multi's offer was tempting. Seeing and being everything. But after accepting that offer, what would be left? No surprises, no expectations, no hope. Nothing. No choices.

And life was being able to choose.

He could accept the multi's offer. He could also keep trying to find Rachel. Or he could try to live with Liya.

Yes, he thought. It would be possible to once again hide, or at last destroy, his memories. Yet again, he wondered why he had never taken the final step, once and for all destroying all memories of Rachel. They had been waiting for him, across centuries over and over again, he'd returned to them, getting caught in searching again – searching and longing, hope and despair. At least on Shylock, the dreams had led him back. Rachel had been there, far down in his subconscious. He wondered if it would be possible to reach such memories and destroy them. Nobody had tried before, but Jack had charted unknown territory before.

Then he remembered that returning memories also were caused by interference from other Jacks.

Cowards, he thought of his twins. Just going with the current.

He could use drugs – he had no idea of which ones, but that would be easy to find out – and create memories where he was looking for somebody else and not for Rachel. He could forge a diary. He could write the story of himself, truthful or forged – and as he thought that, he realized that it was possible and that millions of copies of him, and of others, already must have written every conceivable version of his life.

He might try, he thought, modifying his genes. Find if it was possible to manipulate on that level: removing his obsession with Rachel from his genome. Maybe letting himself be drawn to Liya instead.

But that would also be an escape. Liya, he knew now, was just an escape from Rachel: somehow, Liya was Rachel's less alluring sister, an understudy, somebody he went to when he missed Rachel.

And deep down he knew that he would never seriously try to break free. He had never destroyed his memories; he would never be able to leave Rachel, or his vision of her, behind. That vision had grown into something larger than life, the spoiled girl becoming his main goal in life, even after learning who she really was – and yet he couldn't just discard her. She had shaped his life, for better and for worse, and he neither could nor wanted to be anybody else.

No, he thought. New bodies, modified senses, sure. But never changing myself. Who I really am. My soul.

I refuse.

Never, he thought. If only because the multi had the vanity to tell me what I would do. Not what I could or should do: it told me what I *would* do.

But I am human. I can choose.

I must be able to choose, he thought. Since I can imagine it and It doesn't break any natural laws, it must be possible, and so it must happen somewhere in the multiverse. Why not here?

What do I care about flaws in the multi's world?

He wondered if the choice of one single human being, just one individual among all the septillions and octillions of editions of everybody who ever lived and would live – if that single choice could really mean anything. Maybe it was like that old disease, he thought, cancer: one single diseased cell could grow and become a tumor. Maybe the seed that would destroy the multis was himself; maybe the tumor would spread from him to world after world, from human to human, from creature to creature in countless universes. And this might already have begun; it might have been why the multi became so unusually blurred when Jack asserted his free will. Maybe that was the moment it spread, he thought; maybe it didn't happen just to me but to millions of me; maybe that was what made the multi so anxious.

Maybe that was why I met a multi of Rachels instead of myself.

And what if I change my mind? he thought. Will I do that? Can the multi be right – will all creatures in the multiverse, conscious or not, finally unite in one single multiverse mind, one timeless moment?

The multi seemed to believe that.

But the multi and its equals weren't almighty. If they had been, they wouldn't need their little lies to convince humans.

If multis were the sum of all human beings, and if a few millions of Rachels from different worlds could manifest themselves as a "Rachel" multi when they thought this necessary – would that mean that they must finally reach the eternal moment? Or was that just a plan? A dream?

Jack was exhausted again. He tried to think. He got to his feet and looked out over the temple.

Suppose the multi was right and could unite with all other beings in the multiverse into some kind of god. Some kind of higher being. Why, then, would they have to work to reach that state? The multi had said many times that the multiverse was a fixed unit where all possible snapshots existed side by side, in that never-changing now that the multi wanted to attain.

In that case, it should already have happened.

Not to me, Jack thought vaguely; I am a human being and I fall through time.

But to the multi it shouldn't be like that. She, they, it, should know what will happen. It shouldn't say "To be certain, absolutely certain, is impossible."

Changing an eternal multiverse would be a paradox. And paradoxes don't exist in the multiverse. What seems like paradoxes, like the time traveler giving William Shakespeare a book with his plays, aren't paradoxes in a multitude of worlds.

Then he saw it. He staggered and sat down again.

If changing the multiverse was a paradox – but the multi still wanted to do it – and if the paradoxes in a single universe could be resolved in the multiverse –

In that case, the multiverse could change. Not one single multiverse, because that had to be fixed. Frozen in its eternal moment.

But one of *many* multiverses could change, resolving the paradoxes on its higher level.

Meaning there was a multi-multiverse –

In such a place, a god could create itself. But how, Jack thought, could the multis in his own multiverse benefit from that? Would the eternal moment be mirrored in all other multiverses – like Shakespeare's plays being delivered to him in worlds where he hadn't written them yet?

Jack felt feverish. His hands trembled.

In that case, his mind relentlessly told him, the multi-multiverse must exist as a part of something even bigger.

The ladder of multiverses could be infinite: to avoid paradoxes there must always be another level, a higher one.

The divine creatures formed by all the multis in every multiverse could merge into higher forms in a multi-multiverse. And so on.

And according to the multi, this must mean that there were no flaws anywhere.

That Jack had to give up Rachel.

He got to his feet and walked, almost reeling, to the kitchen. He drank a big glass of water. He thought about opening a bottle of wine but didn't. He was addicted, but not to alcohol.

He thought: People can say no to their equals. They can refuse to serve a king, or even to do right. And I refuse. *Non serviam.* I even refuse to obey Rachel.

The thought cheered him. He shaved carefully before he went down to the river to swim, long and lustfully, in the cold water. A simple pleasure: he could easily modify his body to repel dirt and stop his hair growing. But simple pleasures also were a part of being him.

I might be the only one doing this, he thought, dazzled by blinding sun reflected from the white enamel. Millions of copies of Rachel, negotiating with millions of copies of me, have worked for years to prepare me, soften me, to make me follow their plan. I may be the single Jack in the multiverse still resisting, the one they had planned to convince today. Now, they're in an emergency meeting.

Wrapped up in themselves.

When Shylock turned out to be inhospitable, Jack had had his idea. He had suggested that they should stop being careful with terrestrial DNA and instead just shovel it in, see if it was possible to change the very basis for life on the planet. The group hadn't listened, Jack had given up, soon leaving the planet; and a few years later, life had run amok and killed the colony.

I shouldn't have given up, Jack thought. The many may not always be right and the voice crying in the wilderness is wrong.

I refuse to obey the many, even if they are Rachel or myself.

Jack left the water. He shivered and his skin had goose bumps. Insects buzzed, around him and in googolplexes of other worlds. He would sit here for a while, letting the sun dry him and warm him, before he went up to the temple to resume his search for Rachel.

§

This might be his demise, it was quite probable that it would be his demise, but he wasn't worried. Even before he left his sun-warmed rock he started feeling that well-known thrill: he could try doing *that*, or *that*, or working in *that* or *that* way.

He had a goal. This pleased him. All his life, he had needed goals to strive for. With the multis, he would have reached the final goal. Nirvana, he thought, the end of all craving: he would be like the listless people of Hawaii, except that his never-changing existence wouldn't be filled by holos and virtuals but by aspects of reality. But the listlessness would be the same: the indolent acceptance in a world where anything could happen, where everything actually happened. Which meant that nothing at all happened.

No, he thought again; I don't want that.

He already felt the addict's craving for the rush: going into a new world. The fact that he would be disappointed, over and over again, didn't matter.

If he was going to his doom, he welcomed the journey. And if the multiverse, his multiverse, was created to make the multi's eternal moment stand or fall with Jack's decision – so be it. The multi had one opinion of Jack's destiny. Jack had another.

His mind was finally made up. He was happy.

He would meet nice and unpleasant Rachels, thoughtful and reckless, happy and wistful. They would exist in worlds of starvation, of poverty, of slavery and freedom, of affluence and of wastefulness. While the sky above his temple turned from night to day and back again, while the seasons slowly crawled from dazzling summer to blue midwinter, year after year, in body after body, he would chase Rachel in thousands of universes, like a flying Dutchman whose only goal was the journey itself; different versions of Rachel, dark and blonde, evil and kind, would only be extras that he passed in his hunt since none of them ever could even come close to the idealized dream he chased. He would meet Rachel, searching for him; he would know what it was to be rejected, to realize that he had laughed in the wrong way or failed to be sufficiently attentive when he listened, that he had let her down or forgotten something; he would experience this over and over while he chased impossible perfection. Over and over again he would believe that he had finally found her, as she would believe that she had finally found the right Jack. But after a few days or weeks or months the set pieces would crumble. The bubble would burst. One of them, or both, would wistfully explain what was wrong, or leave a letter, like Liya had done, or just disappear, as Jack had done so many times. They would begin their hunt again, for the thousandth or ten thousandth time, in their hundredth or ten thousandth body. And all over the multiverse countless versions of them, the ones already united into multis, would study their wayward twins and haughtily shake their millions of heads: What did we say? They should have known it would end this way! But to Jack, this single edition of Jack, and to the copy or copies of Rachel and himself that may have chosen the same path or were going to do it, neither failures nor the patronizing majority would matter. He and his equals would tirelessly continue their search. As his body grew more and more gaunt, more haggard from neglect and malnutrition, as hair and beard grew down his chest and back, every failure would just egg him on. He would discover new ways of searching, new places, new methods, and start over again; as long as his body held out. Over and over again he would be found dead; his sons or somebody else would build a new one and transfer his memories to it. And notwithstanding which memories these were, the interference would make him dream of Rachel again, of Rachel's eyes, and everything would begin again. In one way or another. But one day, he knew, it would end. One day, his sons and everybody else would forget him. The temple would crumble into piles of yellowing enamel. One day a vessel in his heart or brain would explode for the last time and it would be over. He would never reach the multiverse and eternity. He would sacrifice the chance to become and be everything, the opportunity to both unite the multiverse and be a part of a united multi-multiverse; he would reject all this for an impossible dream, to search for something that he had found so many times that he knew it could never satisfy him; he was sacrificing eternity for this dream, embracing his own ruin. But the choice was his own. Like the Egyptian queen he followed his own will. And by now he knew that the choice he had made, letting himself stay in his meaningless dream, was his only path to freedom. That the rushes in the never-ending choices gave him what he wanted. That his only peace was in the search for peace.

KG JOHANSSON

KG Johansson was born in the fifties and grew up with rock music which became an important part of his life. In 2005 he became Sweden's first tenured professor in rock and roll, and since 2006 he's been writing and playing full-time: science fiction novels, young adult novels, film scripts, opera libretti and music books. He has translated works by authors such as Arthur C Clarke, Samuel R Delany, Ursula K Le Guin, Joanna Russ, Dan Simmons and Neal Stephenson into Swedish. The winner of several awards and short story contests, KG Johansson is today one of the foremost authors of speculative fiction in Scandinavia.

kgjohansson.se   affront.se

Googolplex

© KG Johansson, 2015

Affront Publishing

Cover illustration by Andreas Raninger

ISBN 978-91-87585-35-7

www.ingramcontent.com/pod-product-compliance
Lightning Source LLC
Chambersburg PA
CBHW060359030726
47497CB00003B/786

9 789187 585357